Back in the Game

All or Nothing Book Two

RENÉE A. MOSES

GussyFlo Publishing

ONE

Airen

"Baby, talk to me. What's wrong?" I asked. My next thought was that something had happened with the girls, but they were giggling loudly upstairs in Ariyah's room. Whenever her door was open, you could hear everything. I made sure not to be too loud as I questioned my lady again about her sour-ass mood. *Who the fuck did something to her?*

"Khaliyah...You gotta give me something here. I can't help if you won't let me in on what the fuck is going on. Babe, please?"

Khaliyah stood there with her eyes studying me. Her mind seemed occupied, but her focus was on me. She broke away from my gaze and raised her hands to her stomach level, then opened her mouth. Nothing came out. She scrunched her face in confusion, then in what could only be classified as disgust.

I clasped my hands behind my back because trying to touch her was out of the question. With every step forward, she'd take two steps backward. Her voice finally made a sound, but no words.

God, what is going on?

"You..." She stopped for a few moments.

"I what, baby? You're scaring me."

Khaliyah laughed with an arrogance that irritated my soul. "Scared? I just saw a fucking ghost. I must have. Because what kind of sick motherfucker would lie about a dead wife? Who would tell his daughter that her mother is in heaven?" She asked calmly. Not loud enough to travel upstairs but clear enough for my ears.

"Khaliyah, I don't know what you're talking about. Walk me through this. What is—"

"I saw her, Airen! Your wife is alive and well."

"I think you're mistaken, baby. This all has to be a misunderstanding. You know me."

"I don't know shit, Airen. Your wife approached us at the mall. She was slimmer than in Ariyah's pictures, with shorter hair and a tattoo on her neck. I'm not crazy. She hugged Ariyah and called her Baby Doll."

It was my turn to freeze in place. My throat instantly lost all moisture.

Tattoo on her neck?

The thought of whom Khaliyah described knocked me back a few steps. I placed my hand on my head, massaging my right temple, trying to keep it together.

Everything was finally feeling normal. The past was where it was supposed to be—behind us. I found my forever in the woman before me, yet she'd gotten a glimpse of my past I'd convinced myself I outran. I pushed it so far down in my mind so that I could be happy again. I'd forgotten a major part of why I stayed hidden for so long. Three years wasn't long enough. Yet the last few months made it feel like a decade ago.

My chest tightened as the reality of my past came crashing into my future. There was no hiding or turning back now. Khaliyah was with me, and I didn't want to lose her over this. I didn't lie to her. I shared only what I thought was relevant until now.

I let my knees falter beneath me as my mind filled with memories, mostly bad ones. The promises I'd made to myself when I left Arizona. Khaliyah successfully shattered the walls

I'd built around me. Those walls existed for a reason. Now, everything was exposed. I sat down in silence and dropped my head, trying to wrap my mind around all that could happen from this moment on. Khaliyah slowly made her way to me, knelt, and shook me. I heard sounds coming from her mouth, but I couldn't distinguish the words.

I finally opened my mouth and released the one thing that had played continuously in my head for the last minute.

"She found us."

Khaliyah looked like I did moments ago, but for a very different reason. Before I could gather my thoughts and process my next moves, I quickly approached her and placed a hand on each side of her face. "Khaliyah, I understand how this looks. There is an explanation. Do you trust me?"

Our eyes locked for a few moments of uncertainty. When Khaliyah nodded, I could breathe again. After leading her into the den, we sat on the sofa.

"Ariyah's mother is dead. I did not and would never lie about something like that. The woman you saw was Mercy's twin sister, Grace." Khaliyah's eyes widened. "Yes, she has an identical twin. I didn't mention it because I left those people in my past."

"Why?" she whispered with a cracked voice.

"That would require me to uncover painful details. I just don't—"

"Airen, you say you want me. You want to be a family. I cannot enter another commitment without the complete story of who you are. Whatever you're trying to run from has clearly caught up with you. Is it fair to still leave me in the dark?"

I lowered my head while she spoke, considering every ounce of truth in her words. "It's not." I thought I had more time to ease into this conversation after we'd gotten further into our relationship. My past wasn't one that should veer us off track. I didn't want to go all the way into it unless we were in this forever. In short, I explained, "I had every intention of sharing everything. Especially with you. I assumed it would be on my terms and timeline."

"Looks like life had different plans, Airen. Now is as good a time as ever."

I nodded. "You're right, babe. Please forgive me. I never meant for you to get blindsided."

"I forgive you as long as you're straight with me."

I grabbed her hands and kissed each one. "Thank you. I will be." My daughter came to mind. Khaliyah said the woman hugged her. "How did Ariyah react? I need to talk to her, too."

"She was quiet at first. I freaked out. I eventually stopped for ice cream to calm myself down. That's when Ariyah mentioned the woman looked like her mom."

"Damn. I am so sorry." I closed my eyes, reliving the highlights of the last few years. "Being here, surrounded by so much love, I'd slowly forgotten about Grace."

"We're y'all close?"

"Me and Grace? Absolutely not. She was the reason Mercy got hooked on drugs in the first place. Her and her damn boyfriend. Grace was a terrible influence and enabler. Since she was Mercy's twin, her opinions had more weight than mine."

"You blame Grace for Mercy's death?"

Swallowing a few times through the pain of someone grabbing hold of my heart and squeezing with all their might, I released a breath and answered truthfully. "No. I blame myself."

Khaliyah's eyes watered as she pulled me into her arms and held onto me like she wanted to magically remove my guilt and shame. "It's not your fault, Airen. You cannot live carrying that, babe. Jesus!" Her embrace felt like heaven's attempt to convince me of her words—the exact words from everyone who saw this side of me.

The girls' laughter traveled downstairs, and Khaliyah gasped. "What are we going to do about tomorrow? Should we still have the party after all this?"

It was my turn to panic. "Shit." I stood and paced a bit. "We can't cancel it."

"It wouldn't be fair to the girls if we did," Khaliyah agreed.

"I gotta tell Unc and Maya. They are well aware of Grace and her antics. We need a game plan to handle this. Not today, though."

Khaliyah met me and caressed my back. "I understand, and I'm here for whatever you need. I can take the kids out to eat so you can have some time alone. They will pick up on your energy. You're not that great at faking it."

I laughed. "Neither are you."

"I'm better at it than you are. We'll tell the kids you need to get things ready for tomorrow and distract them with a slumber party at my house. It will be fine. Take the night to get your thoughts together."

"Thank you, Khaliyah. I love you."

"I love you."

God, I'm grateful for her love. It's the only way we'll get through this.

TWO

Khaliyah

"I know you fucking lying," Karina said from the other end of the sofa.

"Girl! I wish I was."

The boys were asleep in their rooms. Ariyah was with Aubrey. Earlier, I took them to the girl's favorite restaurant and sent a last-minute invite for Karina to join us in Airen's absence.

After dinner, we headed to the store to pick up food for our impromptu sleepover. The plan was to bake cookies, eat junk food, and watch movies until we fell asleep. Midway through the second movie, the girls were out, and the boys were almost there. Hearing about all the fun they had with the men today was exhausting.

Karina pulled her knees up to her chest, resting her feet on the couch. "Now that I think about it, I do remember stuff about Mercy partying a lot. She *did* have a sister. I forgot about them being twins." She took a deep breath and shook her head as she let it out. "Damn."

"Yeah. It's a lot to process even without having the entire story."

Karina pursed her lips to the side, looking like she had something to say but wouldn't. "What is it, Karina? Go on and say it."

After pressing her lips together, she asked, "Do you trust him? Or trust what he told you so far?"

"I do," I answered with no hesitation. "I simply want to know what really went down. It sorta puts things on pause for me."

Karina nodded. "What about the sister? I know you want to hear his perspective, but what if I looked into the sister?" Her shoulders raised slightly with her head tilted to the side. "Maybe I can find out why she's here. I can check personally at the station. I also have a friend who can dig deeper."

"Honestly, I'm all for it. That info can help Airen, too."

"One hundred percent. I'll hit Auggie up to get what I need to start looking."

"Sounds good." I exhaled slowly after taking in as much air as I could. This conversation alone reminded me that Airen was a public figure. As much as I loved him, did I want all that could come with that fact?

"You mad?" Karina asked with genuine concern. "You called it when you thought he was too perfect." She stretched her legs out on the couch.

"I mean...yes and no. At first, I wanted blood because of what I believed he'd done. I'm not really mad, mad. I just hate that he didn't tell me about the sister."

"An identical twin, at that. I wonder what made him walk away from her family. It had to be bad. He kept them out of Ariyah's life all this time."

"That part." I sat up a bit on the couch, thinking of reasons he'd go to such lengths. "We will talk about it after the party. It sucks that he has to deal with this now. Once he does, at least it'll be over."

"He's lucky he has you. I remember reading some stuff about him. Half of it is probably exaggerated, but his name stayed in the blogs while he was married. It was mostly because of his wife. She was a character, to say the least."

"I'll find out all about it when we have a real sit-down. I cannot move forward with my heart until he lets me in."

"I got your back no matter what. Even if twin sis pops off."

"You always do. That's why I love you. But we ain't manifesting any mess. Whatever it is, I pray it's handled peacefully."

Karina tilted her head forward. She knew more about these people than I did. The temptation to get a heads-up caused me to put my phone in my office hours ago. I'm trying to be good and wait for Airen. His delay had the potential to do unnecessary damage if I hadn't calmed down earlier.

"Can I sleep in your bed?" Karina asked as if she were one of my kids. "My back has been giving me the business lately. This couch ain't gonna work."

"I guess. Only since you're my elder. Simple things are tough on you old birds."

"Heffa, we are two weeks apart!" We laughed as we got up and walked into my room. "On second thought, are your sheets clean? I don't want any sex residue on me."

"Girl, shut up. You ain't gotta worry about that." I pulled the covers back. "At least not yet."

Karina released a low scream, acting all giddy. "You better tell me when it happens. I don't need the details, just the confirmation that you're finally getting some. It's been a minute. Hours. Days. Years. I'm hurting for you." She brought her hand to her chest.

"Really, Rina? You ain't gotta remind me. She knows." I looked down at my lower parts, apologizing in my head for the drought but promising her it'll be worth it once we get there. We felt the goods from behind, fully clothed.

AFTER BREAKFAST with the kids and Karina, I took her car to Airen's. She'd use my truck to drive them all to church and then to Airen's house for the party. Although I agreed we'd talk about everything after the party, I wanted to check in on him.

I parked the car in the empty garage space and let myself in with the key he gave me. I found him in the kitchen at the stove. The smile on his face when he saw me calmed my nerves.

"Good morning, gorgeous." Airen's energy felt sad while he attempted to mask it. He inhaled slowly as our lips connected. Then he pecked me twice before going back to the eggs.

"You have two plates out?" I asked, sitting at the island.

"Have you eaten?" He looked back out of the corner of his eye.

"No." I cooked but had no appetite earlier.

"I didn't think so." Airen removed the pan from the heat and walked to the fridge. He grabbed apple juice and poured me a glass. "You don't eat when you're stressed. Yesterday was stressful. So, eat with me."

I kissed my teeth. "Don't be acting like you know me."

His head tilted forward. "Woman, sit your hardheaded ass at the table. It's a simple meal before the long day ahead."

I did as he said, yet I couldn't help but imagine how much more difficult the day was now that Grace was in Houston. Since it was a sensitive topic for him, I kept my inquiries simple. "Did you sleep?"

"A little." He set a plate of waffles, eggs, and fruit in front of me. "You?"

"Kinda. This looks good." I took a whiff. "I see you put cinnamon in the waffles, and you made the eggs the way I like them." I preferred garlic salt, cracked pepper, and parsley in my eggs. He was a salt and pepper guy. We'd cook our way when we were at our respective homes. Today, he switched it up.

He paused before sitting in the chair next to me. "I may have grown to love your way over mine."

"Interesting." We laughed because he was so adamant about simple being better. I took a bite of everything after he blessed the food. "How are you doing after everything?"

Airen leaned back a bit. "I don't know yet. Part of me is relieved. Grace showing up means I have to deal with everything. God knew I would have prolonged it as long as I could have. I told myself I'd tell you everything, but each day of such joy convinced me that talking about the past wasn't worth it."

"Didn't want to spoil the moment."

"Exactly." He took my free hand in his, facing me. "And babe, I cannot say I'm sorry enough for how it all happened. You didn't deserve to be in that predicament. That's from my neglect of being fully transparent."

I tilted my head at him. "I forgive you. I no longer desire to beat your ass. So, we're good for now."

He burst out laughing. "I deserved that. I promise I will make this right."

"I know you will. We just have to get through this party with all the excitement we had before last night."

Airen swallowed his food before saying, "All I gotta do is think of my family's happiness. You are my family, Khaliyah."

He kissed my hand. I believed him. Every word he spoke. He always came across as genuine when we were together. If this man hadn't had me wrapped around his finger, I'd probably still be pissed. Something in me loved him more than I could even explain. I trusted him.

WE SKIPPED church to get the house together with the help of *Cherished Moments* and a photo booth company we learned about at a festival a while back. I kept the woman's card, and it finally came in handy. This pool party was for our close circle of family and friends. That circle was quite large when we added Victor's clan and friends. There were almost a dozen kids connected to him and his wife.

My grandparents and Karina were the only invitees from my side. Aryiah and Aubrey made friends at school. Since the party was at Airen's, we kept it in the family. I was grateful once I realized how many people we'd entertain today.

Airen and Rochon barbecued. Aunt Maya and Gammy made the sides. We ordered dessert treats and cakes from *Treats by Leah B.* Airen demanded that I enjoy the party like everyone else and let him handle everything. Knowing what he was dealing with mentally, he needed the distraction.

The party turned out better than anticipated with top-notch food and being surrounded by our favorite people. The girls were so grateful; they showed it with many hugs and kisses. We now had two six-year-olds.

Airen couldn't stop me from assisting with the cleanup. All hands were on deck once our guests left. By the time Karina and my family went home, Airen was out of sight. I checked in on the kids after they had taken baths and gotten ready for bed. It was a school night, so we'd leave for school from here in the morning.

I walked into Airen's room before I'd retreat to the guest room for the night. Something told me to check on him since he ducked off without a word. I heard voices coming from his bathroom.

I peeked in to find Airen sitting on the edge of the tub with his phone close to his face. His voice came from the speaker, but his tone was one I hadn't experienced in person.

The look on his face concerned me enough to interrupt whatever this was.

Lord, help me.

THREE

Airen

"Airen, what are you doing?" Khaliyah appeared at my bathroom door.

I kept it open to ensure I'd notice her coming in time. Plan failed. I didn't want to lie to her, so I didn't. "Something unhealthy."

"Unhealthy?" She walked all the way in and sat next to me on the edge of the tub.

I promised to let Khaliyah in, so that's what I intended to do. "Yeah. Not only is today Ariyah's birthday, it's also the anniversary of the last time I spoke with her mother."

"Is that what this is?" Khaliyah took my phone from me. It was a paused video that showed nothing but the ceiling of my home in Arizona. The audio was all that mattered. She hit play. "You recorded it?" She asked when my voice came from the speaker. She immediately paused the video and handed the phone back to me.

"Not on purpose. But I can't seem to delete it."

"Oh, babe." Her arm rested on my back as she pulled me closer.

I dropped my head low. "Yeah," I said under my breath. I gave her the phone. "Here. You can press play."

Khaliyah shook her head and held the phone near my lap. "I don't have to listen to it."

I guided her hand back to her side. "I want you to. You

deserve to know what part I played. If this changes your mind about us, I'll understand. I pray that it doesn't, but I wasn't innocent."

Khaliyah hesitated before swallowing hard. I did not intend to scare her. I was the one terrified to open myself up to anyone like this. Each year on this day, after Ari's festivities were over, I listened to this conversation with Mercy.

The love of my life stood and walked back into my bedroom. She sat on my bed and patted her hand on the spot next to her. I hesitated before obliging. "Here goes nothing," I whispered.

Khaliyah took a deep breath. She pressed play, and the wound slowly came undone.

Four Years Ago

"It's your birthday! I cannot believe you're two already," I said to the camera. "You won't see this until you're older, but even at such a young age, Daddy is so proud of you. You are my world. I'm watching you right now in the pool with Aunt Maya." I turned the camera around to face my baby girl splashing around with her great-aunt.

"My life didn't really begin until I held you in my arms. You changed me forever for the best. I will always protect you. I will always love you. I will—"

A loud knock at the door pulled my attention from the video I was creating. I jogged from the living room to the front door to let whoever it was in. My boys, Izak and Nick, said they'd swing through. I was sure they'd try to talk me out of retiring early. I decided in the middle of the past season. The game was taking its toll on my family life. A price that was no longer worth the damage it caused. I had to make a choice. One more year and I was out.

I pulled the door open to find my almost unrecognizable wife standing in front of me. "Mercy?"

"H-Hey, baby," she said, scratching her arm. The subtle twitching in her neck made me uneasy for a few moments.

Seeing her like this irritated the shit out of me. I set my phone down on the table next to the door. "Where the hell have you been? I haven't seen you in over a month!"

I knew she was alive. Every week I had someone get eyes on her for peace of mind.

Mercy quickly rubbed her nose. "Here and there. Mostly with Grace and Polo." I still only met the guy once, but his name was always in my wife's mouth. From what I was told, he supplied everything Mercy and Grace used.

"Of course. You came here empty-handed? Don't tell me you didn't have money for a gift. My accountant told me about all the money you've withdrawn."

"Money for what gift? I don't owe you anything. You froze my account."

I stared at her for at least a minute. She remained silent, waiting for my response. "Our daughter's birthday. I figured that's why you're here."

"Oh, I'll get her next time. I'm here because I need access to my account."

Standing my ground as family and friends suggested to me, I looked my frail wife in her eyes and said, "No."

"No?"

"Mercy, I love you. But I won't support you constantly shooting and snorting shit into your body anymore. It's no secret that you broke your promise again."

"If you love me, you'd help me. I just need one more time. I promise I'll be the wife you deserve and the mom RiRi needs. Help me. You're my husband."

"Mercy, I'm not doing this shit with you. I'm not enabling this sickness or behavior anymore. I will get you back into the program to get you clean. If you complete that, we can talk about the rest."

"Come on, Airen. I never ask you for anything."

"That's 'cause you never had to! I gave you all I had. I fucking wish I hadn't." I pinched the bridge of my nose. "Did you ever love me? Or did you love what you knew I'd give you?"

"How could you say that? I gave you my body. I gave you a fucking kid that you cried like a little baby to have. Now you mad because you have to take care of her? You thought I was gonna sit around and play the forever pregnant housewife? I have a life too."

"No, you have a fucking problem. I tried to help you. Mercy, I cannot let you do this to us anymore. Our daughter needs you at your best. Yet, you'd rather fuck my teammates and get high every second of the day."

"That happened one time! That's why I hate you. You're too damn sensitive. You don't know how to forgive. Or how to have fun. You can have Ari and this boring ass life."

"And you can have the OD that's coming to you." Hating that I said it, I chose my next words carefully. "If you don't take care of yourself, you will kill yourself. You gotta ease up off that shit and come back to reality, Mercy. For your daughter."

"Fuck you, Airen. How can you say you love me and you treat me like a crackhead off the street? If you love me, you'd help me. I just need this money one last time."

"You said that ten fucking times ago. I'm done. Whatever happens to you at this point is on you. I'm filing for divorce."

"That's fine with me. I never signed a prenup." She crossed her arms over her chest.

"You'll be strung out, barely breathing in some shitty hotel before you get anything else from me."

"I'ma make you regret those words, nigga. This won't take me out. I'm bigger and better than this. I'm taking you for everything you got."

She stormed out and slammed the door. I dropped to my knees, weakened by the feeling it'd be the last time I'd see her face as my wife. We were over, and it killed me. I thought she'd choose me, but I couldn't compete with what she polluted her body with.

"Nephew, you okay?" Unc said from the next room. I didn't know how long he was there or how much he'd heard.

I wiped my face and picked up my phone. When I noticed it was still recording, I stopped it and went back outside with Ariyah.

Once Khaliyah's tears fell, I knew she'd view me differently after hearing the way I spoke to Mercy.

"A week later, I tried to find her. My heart couldn't stand the way things ended. I wanted to apologize and help her. No one knew where she was, so I tracked her phone to a rundown hotel. The last time I found her in a place like that, I almost got shot. So, I took a cop with me for a wellness check. The hotel manager recognized Mercy and gave me a key to her room. She checked in the night before. When I opened the door, we found her unresponsive on the bed."

Khaliyah's eyes widened. "Oh, God. You were the one who found her?"

"Yeah."

"Jesus, Airen. And you torture yourself every year listening to this?"

I shrugged. "I deserve it."

Khaliyah wrapped her arm around my back and leaned her head on mine. "Airen, please do not blame yourself for this. What happened to Mercy was awful, but it was not your fault. You did what you thought was right."

"Yeah, but what I said to her is exactly what happened, Khaliyah." I pulled away, undeserving of her pity or the comfort of her embrace.

Khaliyah grabbed my wrist, forcing us to face each other. She took my hands in hers. "I understand how you could feel that your words somehow made this happen, but in reality, they didn't. Was it harsh? Yeah. Both of you said some fucked up stuff to each other."

"I guess that means that you probably want nothing to do with me now." I got up and slowly paced the floor. "What I did was unforgivable. Trust me, I've tried. You came into my life, and I finally felt free from all this, but it hurts no less. I fucked up."

"So did she. So did I and every other person on the planet. That doesn't make you unforgivable. I still love you. I now see why you carry so much pain. Especially knowing that you blame yourself. But Airen, you didn't give her any money. Yet, somehow, she ended up getting drugs that ultimately cost her life. That wasn't on you."

"No matter how much I tried to convince myself of that, I feel no different."

"Was there a note or something that said this was intentional?"

"No."

"Then, it sounds like her body couldn't take any more of what she put in it. By her last words on the video, she was gonna get clean and come for your wallet. That doesn't sound like a woman who was ready to leave this world."

I thought of that scenario too. I also considered the fact that Mercy could've changed her mind. Maybe she thought about our fight as much as I obsessed over it and ended it. Whichever placed the emotional burden on me was the way I leaned. I should've handled her better.

FOUR

Airen

I WOKE UP WITH MY HEART OVERWORKING TO THE point where I felt I'd forget how to breathe. I clenched my shirt as if it'd slow my racing heart and rolled out of bed. The only thing that came to mind was being on my knees and giving it to God. It was what I taught my daughter to do whenever she had a bad dream.

Once my thoughts focused on Him taking this away, I slowly caught my bearings. My heart rate descended, and my breathing was under control. My wet face from tears was the only factor over which I had no control.

My clock displayed the three a.m. hour. I showered and went downstairs to grab some water. I damn near jumped out of my skin when Khaliyah came into view.

I balled my fists to hide the fact that she almost gave me a heart attack. "Woman, what are you doing down here?"

"I couldn't sleep."

I took a glass from the cabinet and filled it halfway with water. "Bad dream?"

"No. At least I don't think so. I don't remember dreaming. I just started tossing and turning. Then someone tapped me on my shoulder. Part of me wanted to jump into bed with you. That scared me." She laughed at herself. "I figured walking around and praying would help a bit. I ain't got time for no ghosts."

Usually, I would've found her statement amusing. After the dream I'd had, not so much. A minute passed in silence. When I still didn't speak, Khaliyah looked concerned.

"Is everything good, Airen? You seem a bit spooked yourself."

I cleared my throat. "I kinda am."

"You want some tea or something to eat. I'm up now. Whatever it is, we can talk about it."

I declined her offer and walked with her to the den. We sat on the couch with only one lamp on. "So, when we first met, I had a dream about you."

"Really?" She perked up a bit, then narrowed her eyes. "What kind of dream? It better not have been anything nasty."

"It was literally the night I met you. I mean, you was looking how you was looking. How you always be looking." I nudged her. "I couldn't help myself, apparently, because we were going at it, and you were doing your thang. Little tricks and shit with your tongue." Khaliyah's mouth fell open. She even hit my shoulder. "What? I can't control my dreams. I wish I could, since it took a turn I couldn't shake for a while."

I described the dream I had last year. It wasn't one I'd ever forget. I watched the smile dissolve from Khaliyah's face.

"What did she mean by you didn't love her enough?" Khaliyah was as perplexed as I was when I first had the dream.

I shrugged, not having a clue because I did my part with Mercy—except for our last encounter.

Khaliyah hummed as she thought about it. "Maybe deep down, this was your subconscious confirming your fears. Not that it's true, but you keep saying it's your fault. That last conversation with Mercy still has a hold on you."

I shrugged. "It's possible. The part that freaked me out was that Ariyah dreamed of Mercy the same night." I told her what Ariyah told me about her dream.

"So, what you're saying is...I gotta fight a ghost." She giggled. "I'm just playing. The only thing I can think of is that Baby Girl might have the same type of feelings. She told you that Mercy was trying to hurt me in her dream. Ariyah wanting me to be in your lives immediately might have triggered guilt in her as well. She wants a mother in her life, but her mom can no longer fill that role. I'm guessing here."

"That's all we can do. Grace popping up makes everything stand out to me. Like us moving on caused Mercy's family to jump back in the picture."

"So, the dreams were warnings?"

"In a way. It's possible that they weren't about Mercy at all, but about her family reopening wounds. I can't see Grace being back as a good thing."

"You haven't had any other dreams about Mercy since?"

"Last night, I did."

"Oh."

"It's probably why all this is on my mind."

"What happened?"

I explained what I remembered.

Mercy was healthy, glowing even. She sat down next to me on my couch in my living room. She stared at me but said nothing at first. Her eyes watered when she noticed a wedding ring on my finger.

Ashtyn and Aydyn came downstairs, spoke to me, and then went into the kitchen. It was like they didn't see Mercy.

"At least you have sons now," Mercy finally spoke.

I smirked. "Yeah, I do."

"I see you aren't afraid anymore."

"Afraid of what?"

"The truth. You used to hold everything when I left. Your wife," she hesitated and sniffled. "She gets the whole you. You gave me pieces. It was never enough to save me."

"Mercy, what are you talking about? I gave you everything I had. You lacked nothing. You were my wife. My everything."

"Not your everything. Not with your whole heart. If you had, you would have never given up on me. You would've fought for me. This..." Mercy gestured at my house. "This could've been us."

"Mercy, that's not fair. I tried."

She shook her head. "No, Airen. I see the way you look at her. The way you think about her. Your love for her is far beyond what you ever had for me. You'd save her."

"I tried to help you."

She shook her head again. "No. You would die for her before you'd let anything happen to her. You just let me go."

"You left us! You chose your sister. I'm not competing with anyone for Khaliyah. She loves me to my core. My place in her heart, in her life, isn't questionable."

"You never loved me that much."

Khaliyah walked in the door, announcing herself with a singsong voice. Aubrey and Ariyah were both clinging to her, their faces beaming with infectious smiles. She knelt for them to kiss each cheek. Both girls said, "I love you, Mommy." Then they joined the boys in the kitchen.

Mercy's tears fell. "Ariyah doesn't even care about me anymore. She has a new mom."

"I'm not trying to hurt you, but when were you ever motherly to your daughter? Besides carrying her to term and birthing her. You left her, too, Mercy."

The disdain in her gaze toward Khaliyah diminished. Mercy's head lowered. "I didn't want what you wanted." She looked up toward the dark hallway. "She needed me more."

Before I asked who she was talking about, I followed her line of sight. Grace was lurking in the hall.

"My sister was my world. Then she stole it from me."

"What does that mean? You wanted to be with her."

Mercy's shoulders rose and fell slowly. "I had no choice."

"A choice about what?"

"It's time for me to go now. Your wife is coming. I can't be in the way anymore." She rested her hand on my cheek. "You're different. Better. I'm sorry I couldn't love you the way she does. Don't let my sister..." Mercy gasped as she faded a bit.

"Don't let her what, Mercy?"

Grace's hand reached from the dark hall. Mercy's mouth moved, but no sound came out. She stared at her sister and disappeared. As soon as she was gone, Grace's hand pulled back before she disappeared.

"Well, damn." Khaliyah stared at me. "That seems fitting."

"Fitting?"

"Your dreams really are warnings. Grace's hand coming from a dark hall? Lurking, even. That has to mean she's up to something."

I nodded. "Okay. What about the rest?"

"I can only speculate here. It sounded like you needed closure. A conversation like that with Mercy was your mind's attempt to do it. Her last words were probably about what you fear Grace is back for."

"The only thing she'd want is money or to cause chaos. With her around, a shitstorm is brewing."

"What's the worst that could happen? Is she dangerous? Physically?"

I shook my head. "Nah. She wasn't before. More like disruptive. The opposite of peace. It was always drama with her. Lies, mess, unwanted attention."

"Well, babe. If that's the worst she can do, it'll be okay. I'm here. I trust you. She won't come between us. As long as you're honest with me, there's nothing she can really do."

"Yeah, you're probably right."

"On the bright side, maybe she's changed."

I side-eyed my lady. That scenario was not one I'd count on, but I agreed anyway. Grace would have had an encounter with God himself to convince me she's not the same conniving woman I knew her to be.

FIVE

Khaliyah

Tonight was the one weekday designated for all six of us to have dinner at my house. Ashtyn was my sous chef for a recipe he saw on social media. We cooked a gumbo ramen dish that combined my son's love for New Orleans and Japanese cuisine. It wasn't something I'd think to make on my own, but it turned out delicious.

While the kids cleaned up after dinner, Airen and I sat in my backyard. "Y'all should start a channel cooking together. That was too good." The man rubbed his belly like my PopPop did after a fulfilling meal.

I shook my head with a quickness. "Nah, I'll leave that to you and the guys."

"You can do it without your face on the screen."

"I'm sure I can, but I won't. It's not something I want," I let Airen know. I pulled out the envelope that I had tucked under my thigh. "Here's something I want." I handed it to him.

Airen opened the envelope and removed the card. "What is this? It's not my birthday yet."

"I know! This gift has to be given ahead of time." I winked before his eyes narrowed.

He opened the card and found round-trip tickets to Belize with a four-day stay at a beach resort. I planned this a month ago, intending to spend quality time with my man, far away from our children. Now, it became an opportunity to learn more about him and his past without interruptions. Airen remained silent as he read the card.

The man's hand covered his mouth, but I saw it quiver a bit. "This is amazing, Khaliyah. Thank you. No one's ever done anything like this for me."

Ever? I let that go, but it created more curiosity about the type of marriage he'd had before. I was sure Mercy wasn't using the entire time they were together. I wondered what good memories he'd had. He dwelt only on the negative ones. A bad habit we had in common.

"You're welcome! I got this around the time you kept saying you needed a vacation, but felt leaving Ariyah during the school year would be too much to ask. Well, I asked, and our family has us covered. I would've canceled it after last week. Now I see it as the perfect opportunity to put everything on the table."

"Khaliyah, I don't want to ruin a vacation with my past drama."

"Airen Rochon, we're doing this. We really haven't had the time to unpack all that has come our way. You're not in this alone. I need to be brought up to speed with no stone unturned. Look at it as a chance for us to be completely transparent with each other. We need this to move forward."

He carefully put the card and travel itinerary back into the envelope, then stared at it for a minute. "If I'm being honest..." Airen took in a deep breath and released slowly. His eyes traveled up to the sky. "That reality terrifies me."

I placed my hand on his knee. "Why?" I pushed his leg to get him to look at me. "It should be the goal if we want a life together."

"You're one hundred percent correct about that. What if it makes you see me differently?"

I shot off a question to let him know how ridiculous he sounded."Did you kill someone?"

"No!"

"Did you abuse Mercy?"

Airen narrowed his eyes at me, making a thin straight line with his lips. "No, Khaliyah."

"Then the truth will only make me love you more. I will gain a full understanding of what you've endured and overcome by the grace of God. You act like you did something unspeakable. We are not our mistakes."

"I know, Khaliyah."

"Good. So, we're going on this vacation and will return with a stronger bond. No exceptions. Okay?"

"Okay."

AFTER ALMOST TWO weeks of waiting, we were finally here. We barely made it to our gate because of all the other damn people taking ridiculously early flights.

"Lord God, we thank you for our safe arrival at this beautiful destination. May it exceed our expectations," I prayed aloud.

"In Jesus' name, Amen," Airen finished before we exited the vehicle.

Someone assisted us to our beachfront villa after we checked in. The people were generously friendly and accommodating, yet all I wanted to do was take a nap. Getting here already took me out. From standing in lines for nearly three hours at the airport, the movie-length flight, and then another twenty-minute drive.

In all fairness, I had no one to blame but myself. I got distracted by a social media feed full of things to do in Belize. I scheduled some activities, but I didn't want a packed itinerary.

We could select some things from what other tourists have suggested. I saved anything that seemed interesting enough.

"You look like you're about to pass out," Airen said.

"I feel like it, too."

"Nobody told you to research everything about the place until the morning hours."

I shot him with my eyes. "Don't start with me."

When the man we followed opened the door to our villa, my entire attitude changed. My energy renewed as I took in the gorgeous interior, which offered a beautiful view of the ocean from almost every angle.

"Damn! You did good, Khaliyah. This is perfect."

I smiled, showing all my teeth. Impressing Airen was the goal. I knew he had the means to do so much more.

My plans were in place before he basically used Mother's Day weekend to pamper me with the help of our kids. Understanding the depths of his need to show love through action and gifts, I still haven't grown accustomed to it. I'd never been honored by a man on Mother's Day outside of flowers or a gift from PopPop. I wasn't even the mother of Airen's child, yet he made me feel so special and valued as a mother.

"Mr. and Mrs. Luke, is there—" the gentleman barely got out.

"Whoa. It's Landry. Mr. and Mrs. Landry," Airen wrongfully corrected the man. I hit his chest. "Woman, just face the inevitable."

The guy looked at a small piece of paper in his hand and appeared confused. "My last name is Luke, his isn't," I confirmed.

Airen gestured for the man's attention. "Either way, *we'd* prefer if you called her *Mrs.* Landry."

"As you wish, sir. Is there anything else I can do for you?" he asked in his heavy accent.

"No, you've been great. Thank you," I said before the man

left. When he shut the door behind him, I hit Airen again on his arm. "Really? The inevitable?"

"Damn right." He laughed. "Then again, that's if you still like me once this vacation is over."

I rolled my eyes. "Shut up."

He wrapped his arms around my waist and kissed me. "You once thought the drama you had with your ex would scare me away. Once you learn mine, you'll understand my fears."

"No need to fear. Babe, this vacation is to celebrate your birthday and to overcome the life you had before by no longer allowing it to bring shame. You've carried it like you were required to. We've both been through some shit, but we are better for it. We will leave here with an understanding that will strengthen us, not break us apart. Deal?"

"Deal." Airen laid another kiss on my lips. "Now, do you want to explain how the hell I'm supposed to enjoy this vacation sleeping in the same bed as you? Are you trying to torture me, woman?"

My eyes bugged as I sucked in my cheeks. "I ain't even gonna lie. I was not thinking about that when I booked the place. I was excited to have privacy with you."

"Yeah, right. You're trying to test my willpower, and I don't think I'll win."

I grabbed his hands from my waist. "I'd have to give in, too. So I'll be strong for both of us."

The moment the words came out of my mouth, my mind yelled, "Girl, please." I was grateful to God that women didn't have visible hard-ons. He'd catch me in my lie right now. Airen sure the hell couldn't hide his.

"Woman..." He picked me up and had me wrap my legs around his waist. Prickles covered every inch of my skin. Each time he touched me lit my nerves on fire. I tried to keep a straight face.

"This shit will not work, Kay." One peck turned my nerves into an aching throb between my legs. We were in dangerous territory once I took in his tongue. As our tongues swiped and twirled around each other's, our breaths became heavier, hungry even. I released his mouth and dropped my head. I was almost embarrassed at how soaked my panties were.

Airen lowered me enough to feel his dick beneath my ass. Feeling him made me forget my promise to myself. I rose my head and saw his closed eyes as if he was fighting in his mind like I was.

I bit and tugged his bottom lip as the throbbing between my legs grew more intense. He held the back of my head while still keeping me up. His hand pulled me closer and he filled my mouth with his needy tongue. Once I moaned, Airen broke our connection. "I'm not gonna make it sleeping next to you."

My plan was backfiring on me. No kids around would allow us to have uninterrupted conversations and learn each other on a deeper level. In all the excitement, I'd forgotten that having them around forced us to be on our best behavior.

We'd been together for months. When we went out, we were in public. When we had family time at home, the kids surrounded us. We had played it safe for so long that it never occurred to me what it meant to remove the buffer.

I hopped down and stepped back. "Oh, this is gonna be hard."

"As fuck." Airen adjusted himself.

We explored the villa to change the atmosphere. It was spacious, with an oversized couch in the living room. All of this was for his birthday, so I told him, "I don't want you to have to sleep on the couch. You can take the bed."

"You are not sleeping on the couch. I will. It will be fine."

"I mean, we can try it one night. The bed *is* big enough. We're grown. We can handle this."

Airen took my hands and rested his head on my forehead.

"Khaliyah, I know I'm nice and respectful. I love you, and I adore you. That doesn't mean that I don't want to fuck the shit out of you. Like every time you are in my presence. You give me too much credit. We *cannot* sleep in the same bed."

While his words matched my thoughts, they did nothing but exacerbate the situation. To be desired by this man became a weakness, especially when he had no problem saying it out loud. I had a silent remedy in my suitcase that I desperately needed at the moment.

Pulling away from him, I swallowed hard. "Um, I'm gonna take a shower and get dressed so we can have lunch. Let's just start there. Tonight, we'll figure out the sleeping arrangements."

I rushed to my bag, grabbed my clothes and my lipstick-disguised vibrator, then ran to the bathroom. I turned on the water to mask any sound I made as I pressed the device against my panties. With the way my clit throbbed, I couldn't even start fully naked.

I'd set myself up for failure. It had been less than an hour, and I couldn't keep it together.

Way to go, Khaliyah.

SIX

Airen

"Wʜᴀᴛ ᴛʜᴇ ꜰᴜᴄᴋ ᴡᴇʀᴇ ᴡᴇ ᴛʜɪɴᴋɪɴɢ?" I ᴀꜱᴋᴇᴅ aloud, washing my hands after cleaning myself up.

Minutes ago, I sat on the floor on the side of the bed furthest from the bathroom door to make sure Khaliyah wouldn't catch me rubbing one out. My shit hurt from trying to get to her. I needed to be close enough to hear the shower turn off.

Once she turned the shower on, I had at least ten to twenty minutes to get this out of my system. That was more than enough time.

Sex was definitely on my mind around her, but we'd done a great job of not allowing the temptation to go too far. With essentially nothing in our way, it proved to be much harder than I expected. This was only day one. Hour one.

Khaliyah took about fifteen minutes in the shower, then I took mine. We had lunch at a local restaurant. The food was cooked to perfection. We kept the topics light and people-watched. I loved how much of a goofball Khaliyah was. You'd never guess by looking at her. She wore a tough mask when she didn't know you. Now, I got to witness the best of her.

When we got back to the resort, we took a walk on the beach. How could we not? It was a warm, breezy day. Khaliyah's perfectly thick, short legs hid in a long sundress. I noticed the ankle bracelet I bought her after she mentioned how cute they looked on other people. I bet it didn't look this good on anyone else.

My mind wandered to a vision of her ankle bracelet in the air, sliding up a bit because I was comfortably between her legs. First, my head, since I've been craving the unknown taste of her love on my tongue. Then I felt her soft inner thighs on each side of my bare hips, and I dug deep into the one place I have yet to indulge. I heard the jingle of the charms on her ankle bracelet near my ear as I'd have her legs on my shoulders.

The silence brought me back to reality, hoping she hadn't said anything that required a response. My ass didn't hear a thing but the imagined jingle.

Khaliyah stared out at the water, looking like a goddess with her long braids tied up in a bun. Her skin glistened in the sunlight. "This is exactly what we needed. I love it out here."

"Says the woman who hates being outside." I got nudged a few inches away but quickly returned to my place near her. "It's beautiful. However, it will never quite compare to you."

Khaliyah stopped in her stride and looked at me like I had just lied to her face. "You know what?" She stretched her fingers out. "Thank you."

I dramatically brought my hand to my chest. "What? She took a compliment? Who are you? Stay with me forever." I took her hand and pulled her to me. Seeing the top of her head was hilarious. If there was one funny comparison between her and Mercy, it was their height. Khaliyah was barely over five feet. Mercy had some inches on her. I kissed her forehead when she looked up at me. "I mean it. Forever."

She smacked her teeth and rolled her eyes. "Here you go." Her legs began moving again. "We'll get there one day. But you have to open up first."

"I will."

"Good! How about now?"

I dreaded this moment for a few weeks. If this was what

needed to happen for Khaliyah to have peace with being mine, then so be it. "Let's do it. Where do you want me to start?"

"Let's start with the easy stuff. How did you meet?"

As much as I didn't want to talk about any of this, I was relieved we didn't jump off the deep end. I described the best times I'd had with Mercy, meeting her in high school after running into her in the hallway. I accidentally knocked her books out of her hand. She accepted my apology and went on about her business. Afterwards, I'd see her everywhere. Eventually, I asked people about her. She was known as the quiet girl with a feistier twin.

We arrived at the villa and sat at the outdoor table. Khaliyah thought it was funny that I almost asked Grace out until I saw her cuss someone out. I turned around just in time to avoid a huge mistake and ran into Mercy again. I introduced myself, and we were inseparable. It was a good time. After a year of dating, I fell hard. I expected to play professionally and assumed I would have a relaxed home life with Mercy. She was my biggest supporter outside of Unc, Victor, and my mother.

My mother was not so convinced. She wasn't a fan of Grace or their mother, Lynne. There was never an exact reason. She would just say it was something about that family that screamed trouble. One day, my mom told Uncle Rochon that Mercy's family would be my downfall. She said that my nose was too wide open to see them as the vultures they were.

In hindsight, I should've taken the overheard advice. Like she'd said, my nose was wide open; Mercy could do no wrong. Her family was a concern, but I figured once I played professionally, it'd be for a team far away from them.

Once we were married, I learned how much of an influence they really were. Wherever we lived, I had to rent a place nearby for her mother and sister. Mercy convinced me she needed her family close, especially during the season. She had a point. Not knowing anyone in a new city would've been hard for her.

I did whatever she asked of me to keep her happy. It worked for the most part. Whenever I was home, she was with me. If we went out, I had someone call ahead to get a private space. We were good, except for our thoughts about starting a family. She was never ready. Even five years into our marriage.

Khaliyah remained quiet and let me talk without asking questions. I didn't realize how much I'd have to say. Any time someone asked before, I successfully avoided the conversation. I should've known I'd be most comfortable talking to Khaliyah. With her, I was never judged. I'd convinced myself that my failed marriage would change everything. I saw how wrong that assumption was.

I talked for a couple of hours, and this woman's regard toward me never changed. My perspective on vulnerability did. I saw it as weak and an easy way for someone to take advantage of me. Khaliyah provided a safe space and even called me out when I was wrong. Not in a way to make me feel bad, but laughing at my audacity back then.

Mercy would always claim that I forced her to have Ariyah, and it would irritate my soul. However, I told her that giving me a child was the least she could do after all I'd gone through with her. I felt justified. When I forgave her for sleeping with one of my teammates, I still held it against her and kind of required her to repay me by doing things I wanted. It was wrong. I was wrong. At times, I wondered if it played more into her wilding out.

"Babe, that's tough," Khaliyah stated. "Not her sleeping with ol' dude to get you back for being seen with his wife. How did the distrust and pettiness get that far?"

"Fools with cameras understood how to catch the perfect angle that told whatever narrative was most pleasing to their pockets."

Khaliyah's features contorted as she asked, "How did running into a teammate's wife at a restaurant and helping her when she tripped turn into people thinking you had an affair? Make it make sense."

"I had no answer back then to convince Mercy otherwise. Grace stayed in her ear, constantly saying I wasn't shit. Roland egged it on. He made shit hard in the locker room, on the field, and in interviews. Nothing I said changed his mind. He thought the best payback was to sleep with Mercy. She blamed the slip-up on being high and heartbroken. Roland caught her at the right time at the right club. They screwed in the damn public restroom."

Khaliyah's eyes bulged briefly. "That must've been embarrassing."

"Definitely. It took the heat off of me and Roland's wife. She was adamant about setting the record straight because we were innocent. Still, it took public humiliation of both our marriages for people to consider we weren't lying. Roland was also vocal that I started it when I touched his wife."

"Whew! Did his wife leave him?"

I shook my head. "I believe they're still together. Eventually, being on separate teams put the right amount of distance between us. Mercy and I moved on. I can't say the same for Grace and Lynne. No one worked. I paid for everything. Mercy insisted that I deposit money into all of their accounts monthly. Luckily, because of Victor, I played my cards right and could afford it. Either way, it fucked with me because they didn't show me any respect. Mercy never checked them. Grace and her mother could do no wrong in her eyes."

I stopped for a moment because other memories flooded my mind about that time after the Roland fiasco. When we moved back to Arizona, I started playing with Nick and Izak. They were exactly what I needed. I no longer had a wife to confide in. It pissed me off to be responsible for able-bodied women who didn't give a shit about me or my marriage, all because they shared the same blood as my wife. Their connection to me put money in their pockets. Mess was good for business for many of the blogs and tabloids. My name lived there because of something Mercy or Grace had done.

August even tried getting Mercy a publicist since she insisted on drawing so much attention. We wanted to switch the narrative. The quiet girl was gone. She wanted the attention, and I wanted anything but. It came with my career. Yet, if I'd known playing football would've led us in this direction, I would've chosen a different route.

I wanted my wife. I wanted it to work with her. Grace wanted her party buddy. When Grace finally got into a serious relationship, I assumed Mercy would have more time to focus on us. Her sister still dragged her around with her and her guy. My wife took more trips with them than with me. Even in the off-season, she chose them over me.

Ariyah came after much begging and a bit of guilt-tripping. It was the only way to get my wife to stay her ass at home. She'd have to stop partying the way she was if she carried my child. In the back of my mind, I believed a baby would slow her down for good and give her a sense of purpose. I was wrong about everything, and my approach weighed heavily on me.

Khaliyah rubbed my back after I stopped talking. My mind traveled to Mercy's unresponsive body on the motel's bed.

"Airen, nothing I say can erase your pain or relieve your guilt, so I won't try. I love you and I am here for you." She shook her head. "I would have never imagined that used to be your life."

"Shit, I lived it and still can't believe it. Most people in my position have to worry about vultures outside their homes. It can still be family, though. The type that only reaches out when they want something. My circle was always small. My vulture lived in the same damn house as me."

Khaliyah opened her mouth to say something, but her stomach spoke volumes. We burst out laughing. "Guess it's time for dinner."

"Do we have a choice? That sounded like life or death."

"Shut up!" She pushed my arm, then leaned in closer with pursed lips. I met them for a peck. "I love you. Thank you for revealing your scars. I know this isn't easy, but it's necessary."

"I can see that now. Tomorrow, I'll be the one asking most of the questions."

She pressed her lips to the side. "I guess that's fair."

SEVEN

Khaliyah

The candlelit dinner was magical. We ate at our dining table, enjoying room service and the night breeze from the big open window. Airen's phone played music in the background, so when we finished eating, he invited me to dance somewhat under the stars.

"How did you get here with me?" he asked as we swayed to instrumental jazz. I assumed the confusion in my mind showed on my face. He laughed. "I mean to say you are a remarkable woman. It baffles me that no one cherished and adored you the way you deserved."

I shrugged. "I wasn't always this person. I had to work through a lot to love myself again. That's who you see now. Maybe who I was before was not worth all that you think."

"Nah. I refuse to believe you weren't worthy of being given the world. I see it in the way your children love and respect you. They love being around you. Your family speaks so highly of you. As much as I love you and am grateful to have you now, I can't imagine any sane man ever letting you go."

"You say that now, but at one point, I was so lost in people-pleasing. I took what I could get and figured that was all I'd ever deserve because I didn't fulfill all that my then-husband needed from me. I was pretty pathetic."

"Khaliyah, you are not pathetic."

"Well, that's where I was back then. I honored the gravity of marriage. To me, it was supposed to be forever. I prayed so hard for that negro to see me as valuable and for his heart to change toward me. God was like 'nope'. But in that pain of rejection, I found strength in God. I changed. My heart toward myself shifted because I put more value in what God said about me than what my ex did."

"That's what I'm talking about." He smiled and spun me a bit as we continued to sway to the music.

"It took a lot of heartbreak to get to that point. I still believed that he'd see me in a different light and choose me again. I was dead wrong."

"We got it right this time around."

"Boy! How can you be so sure?"

"Don't worry about how, just know that I am. You are it for me. With our pasts being as painful as they were, I'd do it all over again to get to this moment with you. We needed the lessons to build character and strength. Those same traits that opened our eyes to each other."

"You may have a point." I looked up at him, comforted in his arms. "If I had met you while you played ball, I would've run the other way."

"I bet you would've. Timing is everything."

"Facts!" I tilted my head to the side, getting a better view of the sexy specimen before me. "I love you."

The smile on his face shot warmth throughout my body. "I love you more."

"Gotta be a competition with you."

"Not really. I get to say this because I am in pain right now, but I don't want to let you go."

I knew exactly what he meant because the moment we touched, his dick grew. I couldn't ignore it, but I wasn't going to point it out either. "We can call it a night. I don't want you in pain." I laughed.

Airen lowered his face to mine. "You ain't gotta laugh, woman." While his forehead pressed against mine, his hands slid from my lower back, over my ass, then to the back of my thighs. He gripped them and lifted me with no problem, which was impressive in itself. I wasn't a small chick.

With my legs around his waist once again today, I narrowed my eyes at his intentions to get through this trip without sex. Pulling me up like this was not a move that would work in our favor. *Was he trying to torture us both?*

"Airen, why do you keep—"

His lips shut me up. My heart tried to reach his. It pumped so hard, it hurt. Airen's tongue tussled with mine and I'd forgotten how to breathe. How could a kiss make me want to give him everything I had? Every part of me. This man's lips had me ready to submit under his leadership, no questions asked.

One of his hands gripped my ass tightly as his other rose to the back of my neck, pressing our connection deeper. With my arms on his shoulders, I lifted myself up and down his torso as I sucked his tongue. Every inch of my exterior was on fire. My interior wanted to ignore every prayer to abstain.

I pressed my covered-by-a-thin-layer center into his abs, wondering if he could feel her pain. The pulsing pain. Gripping my thighs around him as tightly as I could, I whispered, "I want you now."

The man said nothing with his low, intoxicated lids as he slowly brought me down until his bulge brushed against my ass. He lifted me enough to slide me down even further. His dick was right there! Right at my barely hidden opening. His mouth crashed into mine again as he sat me on the counter in the kitchen.

With heavy breaths, Airen licked my lips, then my neck, going further to my cleavage. Once he bit the top of my breast, I knew we'd finally do what I'd wanted to for too long now.

Waiting was admirable, but I didn't give a fuck at the moment. All I wanted was for him to fill me to the brim and have me screaming loud enough to drive the nearby sea life insane. Because from his imprint alone, he'd fuck me delirious.

Airen uncovered my left breast and took it into his mouth. "Mmmm, baby," I dragged.

His hands were up my dress, on my thighs, gripping me inches from where I wanted him to devour me. I scooted closer to the edge to remove any inkling of hesitation on my part. This was happening.

When his thumbs moved to the creases of my thigh and labia, he squeezed me harder and growled, "Fuck!" He released me.

"What?" I asked, trying my hardest not to whine. "What's wrong?"

"Khaliyah, we can't do this. I promised myself I'd wait."

FUUUUUCCCKKKK!!!! I gritted my teeth and hopped off the counter. "Fine."

We got our breathing back on track before he spoke again. "Baby, I'm sorry. I'm really trying here." He placed his hand on my hip. "You mad?"

I moved it away. "Yep!" I stepped away from him without eye contact and said, "I'm going to shower and go to bed."

"Khaliyah, wait. Please don't be mad."

"Don't worry, it won't last long. I forgive you already. I love you. Goodnight."

Once I got behind the bedroom door, I locked it. I found my discrete toy, got on my knees on the floor, and placed it on my bean. It immediately took the pressure off. She wanted to be touched, and if not by my man, this would do. I arched my back even more as I pleasured myself. I didn't muffle myself one bit. He'd hear every moan and utter I made. I didn't give a damn how it'd make him feel or how it made me look.

After I came the first time, I took everything off and lay

across the bed, spreading myself wide, feeling the cool air from the AC that had just turned on. Before placing my dickplacement against my love pocket, I noticed the shadow of his feet at the bottom of the bedroom door.

"Ahhh!" came out loudly as I pressed it to my sensitive nub. I moved it in circles around my clit, enjoying every sensation audibly. "Shit."

I noticed that the foot shadows merged into a big one as Airen obviously slid down the door. The knowledge that he was listening turned me on even more. I didn't care if it was music to his ears or torture. It took only two more positions for me to hit my last one. My eyes were barely open. I glanced at the door, and the shadow was gone.

As exhausted as I was, I needed a shower before bed, and so did he. After I got cleaned up and in my pajamas, I walked into the living room to let him know the shower was free. He gathered his things and headed to the bathroom. Once he was next to me, he stopped. "That shit wasn't fair."

I shrugged. "It was to me." I tapped his chest. "I feel so much better now. I told you I wouldn't be mad for long."

Airen nodded before pulling his bottom lip into his mouth. "I see you." He kissed my shoulder and left.

My wine glass was still half full, so I finished it before lying in bed. A part of me was almost embarrassed about what I'd done. The other was proud. That'll teach his ass to tease me to that extent. If he acted right, I might let him watch next time.

EIGHT

Airen

"How could she do me like that?" was the question I asked myself last night before I shut my eyes and this morning when I opened them. "Damn." That shit had me dreaming of Khaliyah, waking up like a horny ass teen.

Last night, Khaliyah had my ass on the floor outside the bedroom door with my dick in my hand. I had to finish with my mouth closed. I couldn't let her hear what I was doing, although she was doing the same thing.

My imagination about her being all reserved and shy in the bedroom flew out the damn window. Her little performance made waiting to go there that much harder. Khaliyah would definitely drive my ass crazy, and I'd be in that pussy with a straitjacket on. Gladly.

The plan for today was to act as if nothing had happened. If I didn't, I'd be suffering all damn day.

I got up and took care of business in the bathroom. Khaliyah stirred a bit as I came out. "Good morning," she groaned, then yawned.

"Good morning," I replied and quickly got my ass out of her space.

I spoke to the tent in my pants, "Yo! You gotsta chill. She's yours. Just bear with me a little while longer."

I ordered a light breakfast for us, but I was sure we'd eat more once we got out of this villa. Khaliyah joined me in the living room with minty breath and a freshly washed face. She pursed her lips toward mine, kissing me before sitting next to me. She rested her head on my shoulder and said, "I'm still so tired."

"I bet you are. You put it on yourself last night," came out of my mouth, going against the plan I made when I woke up.

The cackle she gave was contagious. I wanted to be mad, but her laugh always got me.

Khaliyah shrugged and said, "Somebody had to."

"That was messed up. I had to sit through all the sexy-ass sounds you make."

"You could've joined." The woman straddled me.

"Khaliyah," I dragged her name, trying not to get fully aroused again. "I thought you loved me."

"I do! But you keep fucking with me. I had to teach you a lesson."

"Fucking with you?"

"You keep starting the fire, then abruptly putting it out. Twice in one day. No, sir."

I nodded. "I'm sorry. But can you blame me? Do you know how you look? How you feel? This shit is hard. I made the oath when there wasn't actual temptation."

Khaliyah sucked her teeth. "I get that. It's torture for me too. We have to be mindful on this journey together. Please don't pick me up anymore. It sends the wrong signals to our bodies."

"Deal. Now get your fine ass off of me before I implode."

Her loud ass laugh eased my frustration. It's the most beautiful, loud yet peaceful sight. Her head falls back, and her mouth opens wide.

Shit! Khaliyah's mouth brought visions of it wrapped around my—

She hopped up. "Let's eat and get out there. I want to play today. I scheduled a boat ride in about four hours and an eco tour afterward. Gotta stay busy so we don't get busy."

"I like the way you think."

———

THE DAY BEGAN with fun adventures and delicious food. We drank and swam, bought things for everyone back home, got showered, and made our way to the resort's restaurant. At lunch, we switched plates. Our tastes were similar, but she definitely preferred more spice than I did.

For dinner, we shared a two-person platter. Eating with Khaliyah was one of my favorite things to do. The expressions on her face when her taste buds were happy were damn near a turn-on. If she really liked it, she'd do a little shimmy that always brought a smile to my face. My favorite, though, was whenever she tried something new. After one bite, she'd look back at the food like it insulted her, then go in for another. That meant she found a new favorite. I loved everything about this woman.

So far, we have kept our conversations in the present. Khaliyah told me the plot of a book Karina put her on to. She was excited about her road trip to a book event this summer. I've read many books, but I've never taken trips to meet the authors in person. The way her face lit up while talking about it put an idea in my head. I added a note on my phone for a future project.

I was relieved not to talk about myself for a change, but I'd waited long enough to ask her what I wanted to know. Once we got our desserts, I said, "Can I ask you something?"

Khaliyah looked up and smiled at me. "Of course, Airen."

"When did you realize your marriage was heading in the wrong direction?"

"Ooh!" She put her fork down and thought about it. "I

honestly think everything turned when I found my voice again. I lost it after trying to be accepted by his family. I was in love and wanted to please people who saw me as less than. I would let them do anything, agree to everything, and fall in line. I was miserable. It wasn't always bad, but once it reached that point, it stayed there. He was mean and self-centered. I didn't notice it until after we got married.

"I was all about what was best for the kids, which made him feel like I put them before him. He was right, so I forgave a lot of shit, knowing I wasn't giving him everything he wanted from me. I wasn't his perfect wife. As much as I took, I didn't compromise with my babies. Those decisions pissed him off even more. The disrespect and disregard became too much to bear. One day, I'd had enough. I woke up in a way."

"Damn." I laughed. "You must've been in the same trance I was."

"I really was. At first, Christian was so loving and supportive despite his family's warnings about me."

I raised a brow. "Warnings about what?"

Khaliyah lifted her hand toward me. "Okay, don't judge me." Her lips went inward before she moved a braid out of her face. She finally admitted, "I used to read his texts from his mother."

My head jerked back. Most women searched through phones because they suspected infidelity. His mom?

Khaliyah responded to my expression. "Listen! His demeanor used to change after she sent him messages. I wanted to understand why. His mother had mostly misplaced jealousy about the closeness I had with my family. I visited Houston frequently, and sometimes he tagged along. That woman did not like that at all. When my Aunt Maya babysat Ashtyn first, his mother took it personally, saying, 'How dare we choose my aunt over her? She was the grandmother.' We were in Houston, and my family forced us to have some alone time. We were exhausted new parents.

"I saw a message that said I'd never love him as much as she did, and one day he'll regret not heeding their advice when we met. I mean, we were freaking college students. We fell hard and really thought that could sustain a marriage with all the changes we'd inevitably experience. He initially chose me over them, but it slowly changed. Anything that bothered her suddenly bothered him. Even though he was living in reality with me, he bought into her crazy imagination and coddled her for it."

"Her imagination about what?"

"So, one time she got offended when I wanted my family by my side during the birth of our kids. She held onto those things and constantly reminded him how it made her feel, even years after the fact. I'd spend weekends in Houston with my kids while he stayed behind. That really became a regular thing after Aubrey. I guess during his time alone, he didn't spend it with her. At some point, she assumed her worst fears of not being able to control him with guilt. In her mind, her son spent more time with my family than with her. She blamed me for anything he did or didn't do for or with her. She was tripping. But it took a toll on him, which made him take it out on me."

"Physically?" I asked. My heart sped up before she answered.

"Hell no! Just harsh words, lots of yelling, and possibly intimidation tactics, as he would throw things in anger or run up on me. He'd tell me I didn't love him if I didn't do something he wanted. He behaved like a toddler having a tantrum whenever we disagreed. He never put his hands on me, but he had a way of making me feel small and useless. I definitely believed I'd never be enough and that'd be my life forever. He eventually filed for divorce. I don't think I ever would have. I wanted my kids to have their father in the home, but the price kept going up. I feared the damage it'd cause in the long run, so I did not fight him in the divorce. I was relieved that he had the guts to do what I couldn't."

When we held eye contact for too long, she looked away. "What's wrong?" I asked.

Khaliyah shook her head. "Nothing. I'd only talked to Karina about these things."

I finally opened my mouth and said, "Thank you for sharing this with me. I'm glad you regained your voice. I'm proud of you. I'm sorry you had to deal with people like them. It can be hard when you've allowed so much of yourself to be minimized for so long."

"Sounds like you're speaking from experience," she deduced.

I leaned back in my chair. My eyes left hers briefly but returned. "In a way. Mercy did so much disappointing shit. At first, I spoke up because I assumed she'd take my advice. Once I understood that my word, feelings, or reputation didn't mean a thing to her, I kept my mouth shut and let her do whatever."

"What changed?"

"Honestly, I was tired of being in the marriage by myself. Mercy wasn't so far gone that we didn't enjoy each other, but she preferred to run the streets with Grace. I was a homebody. We didn't need the money, but she had become known enough to get paid for appearances at clubs, so that's what she did with her time."

"That must've sucked."

"It did. I eventually convinced her it was time for us to really settle down and start a family. Mercy gave me a lot of pushback. I honestly thought that giving her a different type of responsibility would bring her back to earth, back to me. In my mind, we'd raise babies together, and she'd want to be home more. I was dead wrong about that one.

"She milked her pregnancy to make more money and gave exclusives to the highest bidder. Some shoots required my presence so that they wouldn't give the wrong impression. Mercy knew how much I hated sharing our private lives with the world. She did it to spite me."

"I'm guessing there are some pretty nice pregnancy photos, though."

I dipped my chin at her. "I would've been fine with the ones we took alone. After Ariyah came, I had a good two months with Mercy, spending most of her time with me and our daughter. Grace barely showed her face. Her family blamed me for forcing a baby on my wife. Once Ariyah got her two-month shots, Mercy was gone again."

"Damn. Two months?"

"That's when I realized she really didn't want me, our family, or the life I wanted. She wanted to use my name and money. She'd come home for a few days a week for the first year. Maya was a tremendous help, as was the nanny, because my schedule required me to go out of town for games. It was a lot. By the time our daughter was about a year and a half old, I saw Mercy a few times a month. She looked different every time. I had to make a choice. I ceased the deposits to her and her family's accounts. That was the only reason she showed up on Ariyah's birthday. Whatever was in their accounts had run out, and they finally noticed nothing had gone in for months."

"Goodness."

"The rest you know. Even though it wasn't necessarily my fault, I wasn't a perfect husband. If I'd been better or more understanding, maybe she would be alive. We probably would have divorced, but at least she would still be alive. But on the flip side, I probably wouldn't be here with you."

She shrugged after biting a piece of pineapple. "We don't know that."

"Yeah, I guess not. I want to think I still would've made it to you."

"Of course, you do. You're only intrigued because of what you heard last night."

My eyes bugged before I slowly nodded. "I got something for that."

"I know you do, but you refuse to use it."

This woman!

NINE

Khaliyah

Belize stayed on my mind since we stepped on the plane back home. Airen and I spent a few days apart. We typically saw each other more at the end of the week, so we stayed on that schedule when we returned.

After much recollection, giving myself an orgasm while the man of my dreams sat on the other side of the door was embarrassing. I'd never done anything like that. Airen reminded me almost every night before we got off the phone.

Last night he said, "Have a good night, but not too good. We don't need the kids hearing you moaning and shit."

I came back with, "I'm a pro at this. I can be quiet."

Then he ended it by saying, "That's because I haven't touched you yet."

Like I needed more ammo to take myself down on his behalf. If only that man realized the number of "good nights" I'd experienced since our first encounter. It'd been more in the last year than it had been in the previous five years. I wanted him more than I had ever desired anyone in my life.

PopPop, Rochon, and Airen took the boys to Topgolf. Karina took the girls to the movies. I was sure they'd sucker her into something else afterward. Aunt Maya had a late appointment but planned to meet me and Gammy at my grandparents' house. We planned to have dinner before I go to Airen's for the weekend.

Maya walked in with an extra pep in her step. "At this rate, I might retire early," she said.

"If only you didn't love closing deals," I reminded her.

"Girl! Don't I, though? I'm so good at it, so why not?"

We laughed. Gammy folded her arms over her chest. "Alright, Missy. Don't get cocky. Make sure you give God the first fruits."

"Oh, Mama. You taught me better than that. I always will. He's been too good to me not to honor him first with what he blesses me with."

"My girl. Now, your niece was telling me about her gorgeous trip with her gorgeous man." Gammy did a little shimmy in her seat. "You need to see the pictures."

"Oh, I have. I made her send them when she was there. It was proof of life."

I rolled my eyes. "You act like I wasn't at a resort. You made me share my location!"

Aunt Maya pursed her lips. "Little girl, I don't care if you were at a palace. You were out of the country. I'm gonna worry, regardless."

Says the woman who explored the world with her hubby once or twice a year. They often traveled the U.S., but those big trips were less frequent. She wanted to see the world, but was borderline afraid of it at the same time. Her favorite line was "Everybody hates Americans" or "I wanna see how this country treats Black folk."

One day, I want her to be free and enjoy herself without those thoughts distracting her from the beautiful planet God created. Were there messed-up people on it? Absolutely. However, I liked to travel with a more positive outlook.

I held eye contact with my aunt, deciding whether I was mad at her. "So, you knew everything that went down with Mercy?"

"Of course!"

"Why didn't you say anything about it?" I asked.

"It wasn't my place to tell you anything Airen hadn't shared. All I could say was how good a man he is. Life threw some things at him; he fought back a bit, then he gave up. He deserved much better than what he allowed himself to experience. You were the perfect person to reveal that to him."

"How could you possibly know I'd be what he needed?"

Aunt Maya narrowed her eyes and tilted her head. "After you and Christian turned out exactly how I thought you would, I believed I had a knack for knowing. The same way I know that woman Christian got ain't staying with him for long. People who mistreat others pay in some form. Mark my words, if she has any sense, she won't stand for his insanity."

I leaned back on the couch. "I'm not so sure. She's drinking the Kool-Aid."

Aunt Maya kissed her teeth. "So did you at one point. It wore off. Trust me. It won't last. As far as Airen goes, you are the perfect match. Children, past, and all."

"Ugh! I feel so bad for all that Airen has held onto. I want to help him, but how?"

"Pray for that man, Khaliyah. Cover him. God will show you how to love him well. That's what will help him the most," Gammy advised.

"Yeah, you're right about that. My prayers can be more specific now that he's told me everything."

"Child, I'm glad he finally let someone in all the way." Auntie rolled her eyes. "The man is as stubborn as you are. It's like you both have a thing for punishing yourselves."

"She has always been that way." Gammy laughed. "Khaliyah, you must learn to forgive yourself and move on quicker. I don't want you moping around, holding onto mistakes you cannot change. I hope you've learned your lesson. Dealing with someone who does the same thing can also shed light on your bad habits."

"It's so much easier said than done. I'd give the same advice. But as far as my marriage was concerned, I see that I was too hard on myself. However, we both played a role in its failure. The blame is not all on Christian."

"Well, the second time around, you will do better. This one will last a lifetime. Just you wait." Gammy sang the famous *Hamilton* line and nodded.

"When we get to that point, I believe the same thing." I wouldn't admit it to Airen. Honestly, I didn't have to since tomorrow was his birthday. Everything was set. He'd understand how much he meant to me even without me saying a word.

Aunt Maya looked at her watch. "Let's go eat. I gotta get home at a decent hour to spend time with my man."

Gammy side-eyed her. "You wanna spend time naked."

"That's what I heard," I mimicked one of our favorite *227* characters.

Auntie's mouth was damn near on the floor, then she pursed her lips with her eyes to the ceiling. "True or not, I still want to get back to my man."

Less than three hours later, Aunt Maya dropped us off at Gammy's, then I drove to Airen's. The kids were already there, and I had our weekend bags in my back seat. Spending time with the wisest women in my life rubbed off a bit. I realized I was stubborn and sometimes learned things the hard way.

Life had given me another chance at love with a man from my wildest imagination. Airen was the type of man I'd read about in books. Like, who the hell actually meets and falls in love with a former pro athlete who has a heart of gold?

The man was funny, down-to-earth, responsible with money, thoughtful, and the type of father anyone would love. He raised his daughter on his own. Airen was a good guy. These things didn't happen in real life, yet God made it so.

With so much negative history in our former lives, I

prayed that we'd learn from our pasts. Although neither of us was anything like our exes, patterns and bad habits could still arise. Gammy advised me to pay close attention to my mindset when dealing with the type of man I hadn't loved before.

While driving to Airen's house, I couldn't get the possibility of forever out of my mind. "God, I know you are with me. I trust you. You know what I've been through with Christian and how it can warp my view on things, especially about people's intentions. Please do not let me sabotage what really feels like the chance of a lifetime. Not with my mouth, my doubt, or my negative spirals."

I turned onto the main street near Airen's neighborhood. "Lord, I have a lot of work to do within. Please give me a clean heart and a renewed spirit to accept what you are giving me now. I don't want to compare anything to the past in ways that might push a good man away.

"Whatever Airen still struggles with, please help him heal. I'm sure there is much he hasn't shared. Or at least the specifics. You know every second of his past and how it has changed his perspective on love. We are two very flawed people, healing from heartbreaks. It feels great now, but when things get tough, show us how to navigate it according to your will."

I made it to the gate and used my access remote. "I guess I have to stop talking your ear off. I really want this to work, Father. My boys love him. My daughter adores him and is crazy about Ariyah. I never thought this would be my life. It took a lot of pain to get here. As much as I don't want to deal with certain people, I wouldn't change it for anything. You see all. Everything happens for a reason.

"Having this man, family, and connection as the reward for enduring our pasts shows me it was all worth it. I told you I didn't want to deal with relationships anymore. Thank you for responding with the best relationship outside of yours. Cover us. Keep us. Never leave us. With you as the head, I can finally see a future to rejoice about. A love once unimaginable."

I pulled into the garage and parked. "Forgive me for not giving you my first marriage and for giving up on the covenant I made. Thank you for not letting it be the end of my love story. It's only the beginning. Whatever comes our way, we will follow your lead this time around. In Jesus' name, Amen."

As soon as I finished, the door opened. My man stood there with a smile that tugged at my heartstrings every time I saw it. He was really it for me. I will probably play hard to get, but if he asked me right now in his t-shirt and pajama pants, I'd say yes over and over.

TEN

Airen

ONCE SATURDAY MORNING CAME, I WOKE UP TO breakfast in bed.

Khaliyah and the kids stayed the night so we could all celebrate the morning of my official birthday together. That was my only request. I didn't care what we did or where we went; I just wanted us all together.

After they sang Happy Birthday, I blew out the candle stuck in the heavenly French toast, covered with powdered sugar and whipped cream on the side. It was one of my favorite dishes.

"What did you wish for, Daddy?" Ariyah asked.

I looked at all the smiling faces and told the truth, "It was more like a thank you to God. He's already given me my wish. It's all of you." The way Ashtyn cheesed before dropping his head to hide it made this moment even better. I was so close to having two sons.

None of this seemed real. We'd only met a year ago and started dating at the beginning of the year. Since we saw each other so often before things got serious, I'd already fallen for Khaliyah and her family. Timing was everything, and because we found each other at the right time, other factors didn't matter. This was my family.

"Aww." Khaliyah came over and kissed me on the forehead

instead of my lips. Otherwise, the kids would vocalize their disgust. "Well, enjoy your breakfast."

"I made the eggs!" Ashtyn exclaimed.

"I cut the fruit," Aydyn bragged.

Aubrey didn't want to be excluded, so she told me, "We poured the juice and poured the syrup." She pointed to the small container on the side.

"Miss Khaliyah let us flip the toast, too," my baby added.

"Thank you all. I appreciate every small touch. It looks great, but I want to eat with y'all."

"NO!" Aydyn and Ariyah yelled.

Khaliyah dropped her head, hiding her smile. "The thing they basically revealed is that we have a gift for you. Eat in here. Then we will come get you."

One by one, they filed out of my room. As soon as Khaliyah closed the door, I eased the tray to the middle of my bed. A bed we have yet to share, but I wasn't worried about "if" anymore. That woman was my wife. In due time, we'd share every part of ourselves and our lives.

I stood up and paced the floor. My thoughts were flashes of the recent past when I met Khaliyah and her family. Then, to memories of what life was like before them, when it was only me and Ariyah. I revisited the future I had assumed I'd live—alone and content once my daughter leaves the nest.

Everything changed after one encounter. Our trip to Belize was a dream come true. We experienced unique adventures and tough conversations. While most of what we discussed was our past relationships, we also learned that our mothers weren't part of our lives for two very different reasons. We connected on a deeper level, and I never wanted that tie to be severed.

"God, I know what I want, and I hope it aligns with your plan for my life. My mind wanders to the extreme when things are going too well. This is one of those times. Everything about this family feels right, but I don't want to trust my feelings. I want to marry her, but only with your blessing. Reveal what I cannot see on my own. I want to make the right choice. I love her, but I love your will more. Please guide me, Father. Show me which way to go. In Jesus' name, Amen."

I walked over to my food and pulled the tray close to me.

"Oh, and thank you for this food. Amen."

SURPRISE AFTER SURPRISE, this was hands-down the best birthday I'd ever had. The family served me breakfast and then decorated the living room with the foyer table full of gifts, both purchased and homemade. My favorite was the framed picture of the six of us. There was no way I deserved this much love from a group of people I knew nothing about this time last year.

We spent the day simply watching movies and playing games. I'd gotten a million and one phone calls and texts wishing me a happy birthday. I couldn't have dreamed of a better time. An alarm went off on Khaliyah's phone before she made everyone get dressed. I assumed we'd head to a dinner reservation.

We drove for twenty minutes before she had me wear a blindfold. Once we parked the car, the boys guided me into a building. I could tell other people were around—the sound of moving feet and the not-so-quiet "shhh" that came from across the room.

When Khaliyah removed the blindfold, the room full of people yelled, "Surprise!"

My attempt to suck up the tears failed. Khaliyah kissed my nose and wiped away the tears. "Thank you, baby. I can't believe you did all of this."

"You deserve it and then some. With all that you give, you

should expect this from now on. We are all blessed to have you in our lives. So, we will celebrate your birthday all the way," she told me.

God, this is what I was talking about. The woman I was with for more than a decade never did this for me. A woman I'd known less than twelve months tells me I deserve all of this. Is she even real?

I greeted everyone individually. They took the time out of their day to be here on mine. Some attendees traveled a considerable distance. I dapped up Izak, then Nick, who had his family with him. Victor and his family were in attendance—Unc, Maya, Khaliyah's grandparents, Karina, August, and her crew. Plus, many of her employees who were basically like family.

I was speechless. Not to mention a table full of gift bags. I was a grown-ass man, and I'd never had this many gifts given to me on any occasion. My family had outdone themselves with this one.

For about an hour, we danced, talked, and ate. There was a wall with a projection screen that displayed the night's itinerary. In about fifteen minutes, we'd be playing games, and that's when the party would really begin. Everyone I loved was competitive, so this was sure to be an interesting night. Luckily, Ashtyn and Victor's stepson, Junior, would run separate games for the kids to play. None of us would go easy on them if we played together. Khaliyah understood that and planned accordingly.

I kissed Ariyah and Aubrey on their foreheads after our dance. August waved me over, so I left them with Aunt Maya. We stepped outside onto the lit patio. We hadn't seen each other in person since before my birthday trip, but we definitely dealt with business remotely.

August nudged me in my chest. "I'm so mad at you right now."

"How? It's my birthday. You're here to celebrate with me."

August swayed her neck at me. "So, you meet the love of your life, and now suddenly you agree to everything I've been begging you to do since forever?"

"I thought you'd be happy about doing the show on screen."

"Nigga, I am! I'm mad that it took Khaliyah to make you see how ridiculous you've been."

"How about we focus on the positive? You won't need to find a space in Arizona. We will record at Izak's house. Let's find reasons to put a smile on your face. Frowning will age you."

"So will stress."

"So, now I'm stressing you?"

"Yep. Not the show. I'm excited. We will start the process and create a schedule that minimizes travel. You'd have to record multiple episodes while you're there."

"Whatever you need me to do."

"We can get you guys on other popular shows to promote ours, too."

"Okay."

August side-eyed me. "Oh, this is weird. I'ma have to get used to you agreeing so quickly. What the hell did Khaliyah do to you in Belize? Are you a clone?" She pinched my cheek hard.

"Ouch!" I gently pushed her away from me. "How's that supposed to prove anything, Dodo?"

She shrugged. "You're just different."

One of Khaliyah's favorite passages was 2 Corinthians 12:7-10. On our last two days in Belize, we shifted the tone of the trip. The temptation was real, and my lady pulled out the Bible to help us. That led to the whole Grace situation and my fear of being in the public eye. Even with the show's growing success in audio only, I still hated the idea of any part of myself being available for the world to witness. It changed when we studied this passage and prayed together.

Khaliyah didn't trust many pastors, but the ones she did, she swore by. They were authentic and spoke only the word of God. No self-serving agenda. She shared the few sermon podcasts she listened to. I promised her I'd go to her church with her tomorrow. I watched her pastor when she first mentioned him months ago. It was one of the first steps I needed to take if I was going to walk the faith I claimed to have.

"We talked about the past, present, and future. Khaliyah reminded me that I am covered. Whatever I face in life, God will give me the strength to endure. I must praise him in every situation and circumstance. I wasn't really doing that before."

August looked at me with her usual skeptical expression, then she kissed her teeth. "All this time I thought she really put it on you."

I sucked my teeth. "Everything ain't about sex."

"That means she still ain't gave you none," Auggie spewed matter-of-factly.

"I ain't give her none either."

"Mmm-hmm. Anyway, I've got something else we need to talk about."

"Now? We're at a party! *My* party!"

"Which is the perfect time to catch you in a good mood." August bit her thumbnail. "Sooo, Karina found out that Grace now lives in Dallas. She gave me a number listed for her. I had someone call her so I could speak with her about popping up."

"Auggie, that's not what we discussed."

She pressed her lips together and let her head fall to the side. I shut up and let her talk. "You are like my big brother. I do not care. Grace grabbed my niece and scared the shit out of my soon-to-be sister-in-law. I wanted to sort this out so we can address it proactively. The bitch wouldn't talk to me. She only wants to speak with you. Claiming it's a family matter."

I nodded my head even though this scenario was one of many I'd considered. "Khaliyah and I talked extensively about it. I will meet up with Grace and find out what she really wants."

"Oh, hell no. You don't owe her anything. Yeah, she is technically Ariyah's aunt. I'm putting my foot down with that one."

"And I'ma yank my foot from under yours." Auggie narrowed her eyes at me. I stood my ground and explained, "None of this means I am even open to agreeing to whatever she may want. I don't need her showing up unexpectedly again. It proves she was looking for me and found me. We've gotta end this. Khaliyah thinks it could be a good thing. Maybe Grace has changed after losing Mercy and Ariyah."

"No offense to sis, but she don't know what she's talking about. I was there. You were there. Grace and Lynne didn't give a fuck about y'all when Mercy was alive. All they wanted was your money, and they used Mercy to get it. Were they at the funeral? Did they show up for Ariyah on her birthdays? Holidays? Even her birth? No! I call bullshit. She wants something other than a relationship with her niece. I'd put money on it."

"Look, I agree. But we won't find out unless I talk with Grace. Isn't that what she told you, anyway? Besides, if they haven't changed, I have. I don't hate them anymore. God has been good to me. With all the shit we've been through, we are better than we've ever been. I'm doing this. Give me her info."

"Nope. I will coordinate everything professionally. I'm setting this up like a business meeting. I'm not taking no for an answer. You can meet Grace at my office at an agreed-upon time. I will give you privacy in my conference room. That's final."

"Okay, Mom."

"Whatever. Let's go back in here and enjoy this party. I need some more liquor dealing with your ass."

The moment we stepped inside, my eyes darted to the one woman who made all of this worth it. With her in my corner, this will be another hurdle I'd clear. No matter what, I would not let outsiders or the world steal my joy and peace. I finally found the proper armor to conquer anything and everything. It was time to put it to use.

ELEVEN

Khaliyah

AUGUST AND HER FAMILY JOINED US FOR AIREN'S first time physically attending church in years. Her support of Airen was beyond business. Their bond was beautiful, considering he was an only child, like me. I appreciated the people in our lives who have become like siblings to us. Since she was his sister from another mister, we'd had a chance to really get to know each other.

At brunch, we discussed why Airen should and shouldn't meet with Grace. Ultimately, the decision was his, but August mentioned my influence and how happy she was that I at least had his best interests at heart. We concluded the conversation with a shared understanding of our differing perspectives on the matter. I loved her even more. She didn't hold back how she felt or judge based on that alone. She was a woman who talked things out, and for that, she was becoming a close friend.

After playing hard last weekend celebrating Airen, it was time to get back to work. August contracted me for a few projects at her agency. The woman was about her business. I loved spending time with her because she was authentic and honest. Working with her shouldn't be any different.

My meeting today was with Khanan and Tyree. I'd already had an assignment to design a website for one of August's clients. She'd usually put up basic sites, but now August desired very detailed customization. When she learned about my business, her entire vision for her web presence changed. She'd been sitting on ideas for years because she didn't make the time to flesh them out. That was why she hired me.

Khanan arrived early to discuss design ideas and optimize his business site for better performance. He also wanted to discuss app ideas, which excited me. It'd been a while since a client had requested a mobile app.

When I first met Khanan, I thought he was so handsome and polite. He reminded me of PopPop in his old pictures. He looked like he belonged in our family. Not all black people looked alike, but some of us did.

"I love the punctuality," I told him as he sat down next to me.

"I had to impress big sis." He smiled. "Besides, I'm not tryna hear August's mouth. I know y'all are tight."

"Maybe, but aren't you her cousin?"

"Yeah, on my dad's side. It meant absolutely nothing in terms of business. She made us work to get here. However, she helped us along the way."

"Really? I love that."

Khanan explained how August supported his vision since he and Tyree had graduated. She arranged some opportunities for them to learn and grow, yet never took it easy on them. They had a proposal-writing business for small business owners. The goal was to help their clients get funding for their startups. It had been successful enough for August to bring them in so they could finally scale up.

"We had so many ideas out of the gate, but Auggie made us create step-by-step goals and work them one at a time to prove we had patience and longevity."

"Smart."

"Yeah. She's hard on us because she believes in our endgame. We moved here last year, and she had us working with her more established clients who could afford to invest in their dreams. It's not just about sponsorships anymore. People want to make a difference with what God put on their hearts. We help them organize their ideas and create an elaborate plan to implement each step. Kind of what Auggie made us do."

Tyree entered the room two minutes before our scheduled meeting time. "Y'all already started?" he asked.

I shook my head. "Of course not. You are a part of this."

"Oh, good." He set his bag on the table and sat on the other side of me.

I opened my laptop, which mirrored the big screen on the wall. I asked Tyree about their progress with Airen. August gave me Airen's site as a project. After the announcement, the site will need to accept donations for the rec center.

"Um, you might know more than we do." Tyree chuckled. "We have his mission statement, and the numbers are somewhat ready. It depends on the location he ultimately chooses to lock them in. I'm excited for him and everyone involved. Preparing young athletes with the right mindset to complement their innate skills will ultimately change the game for them. And I mean, it's Airen Landry."

"Right?" Khanan chimed in. "We've worked with other high-end clients and were in awe of the opportunity, but not a future Hall of Famer. When I told my dad that I was sitting down in meetings with one of his favorite football players, he guessed right the first time. Obviously, I couldn't confirm it, but I told him that one day he'd meet the person I was talking about. My dad is a long-time lover of football. Airen is one of his top favorites of all time."

Tyree nodded. "That's the only hard part of this job. You can't always share details about who you're working with. I respect him for wanting privacy because a lotta these dudes be telling business nobody asked for."

I pointed at Tyree. "You ain't lying about that. Well, let's get this party started. Sounds like the world needs this site up and running so y'all can help some business dreams come true."

Khanan blushed. "I like that. We make businesses' dreams a reality."

"Sounds like a new tagline," Tyree said as he wrote it down.

Two hours later, we had the bones of the site's look and functionality. I'd take it from here. I gave them the timeframe when I'd be done, so we can have another meeting to ensure it's to their liking and move forward from there.

August poked her head in the room before coming in all the way. "Oh, perfect timing." She made her way to me after speaking to the guys as they were leaving. "Let's go out for lunch. We need to discuss the *other* meeting."

"Grace agreed to meet here?" I whispered.

"No other option was given. Airen is going to meet us at the restaurant so we can talk about it." She cheesed and snickered.

"What?" I asked as I zipped up my bag.

"Girl! Airen is meeting us at a restaurant. A year ago, ain't no way I'd be saying that. Whatever you are doing, keep doing it. He's so much better with you in his life. There was nothing we could do or say for years to make this man go out in public."

"I didn't do anything. Airen slowly began making those choices on his own."

"Mmmhmm. He may have made the choice, but you were the reason behind his getting over himself. Airen has experienced some shit in his lifetime. Especially since he went pro. Grace was one of the shit-stirrers. Either way, he's different with you. He smiles and laughs more. He's open to new things." August placed her hand on my arm. "Please take care of my brother. I love him with all my heart. Seeing him this way just..." She sniffled and wiped her welling eyes.

"Don't cry." I grabbed a tissue from the box on the side table behind me.

"Sis, these are happy tears. The women in his life kind of fucked him over because of dollar signs. These were women who were there before the money. For you to come in and love him the way you do, I have nothing but love for you. He be talking shit about you not wanting to accept gifts from him. Shoot, I tried to convince him to give me one of your gift baskets last year."

I burst out laughing. "Ugh, not them damn gift baskets. I love the man with everything in me, but he is definitely the type to go overboard. I love simple things. I still haven't used all the gift cards. Yet, he continues to give."

"Girl, enjoy it. Not all men are like that."

"Oh, I learned from experience. I just needed him to understand he didn't have to buy me. As I got to know him as a person, I realized that's his thing. He's thoughtful and caring. Whether he has a little or a lot, he'd still be giving. I have to learn to accept it."

We walked out of the room. "Girl, he said the same about you."

"What?"

"Yes, ma'am. A vacation? The party? You are a giver too, and he is not used to it. I always gotta hear about how unreal he thinks you are. You got my boy wide open."

"The feeling's mutual."

TWELVE

Airen

QUICK TO LISTEN. SLOW TO SPEAK. SLOW TO GET angry.

I repeated the scripture that Khaliyah often used when dealing with difficult people. Well, mainly her ex-husband. August's office assistant's voice came over the room's intercom, informing me that Grace had arrived and would be escorted to where I was.

Quick to listen. Slow to speak. Slow to get angry.

I held onto my lady's hand as she sat firmly next to me. The peace that came over me when her eyes locked with mine before she leaned in to kiss my lips softly was almost scary. It was as if she had read my mind and helped me relax.

Khaliyah reassured me. "It's gonna be fine, babe. I got your back if she pops off."

I chuckled. "Always ready to fight. You and Auggie."

"Only for the ones we love."

There was a soft knock on the door before it opened. August held the door for Grace to walk inside. My chest tightened at the sight of her. All I saw was Mercy and the pain I experienced with her family. August closed the door and left us to deal with this for good.

"It's been a while, brother-in-law," she greeted before taking her seat, if you could call it a greeting. "Who do we have here? I was told we'd be speaking alone."

Keeping my eyes on her every move, I addressed the concern. "Her presence is necessary for us to speak at all, Grace. You don't need to know who she is."

"You don't have to be so secretive, Airen. I remember seeing Khaliyah *Luke* with Ariyah at the mall."

Khaliyah's head jerked to the side, matching my confusion. I asked for both of us. "How do you know her name?"

"A little research. We've been looking for you for quite some time."

"We?" I inquired, hating every word that came from her mouth.

"My mother and I. You remember, don't you? The woman who gave birth to your wife. The grandmother to her only grandchild, Ariyah. A grandchild she'd seen only a few times in what, five years? That's who *we* are."

Grace's eyes were on Khaliyah as if she was informing her of something she hadn't been privy to. At that moment, I was so grateful for Belize. My baby wouldn't be surprised by anything I'd previously withheld.

August walked into the room and sat in the chair on the other side of me. Everyone in the room probably expected it. Auggie could not stand Grace and Lynne. She wouldn't be herself if she didn't insert herself into this conversation.

Grace rolled her eyes. "I should've known you'd be present. You aren't capable of minding your own business," she spewed at August.

"My brother is my business, Ms. Noble." August addressing her by her last name meant she was more irritated than I was. I bumped the side of her leg with mine under the table. She didn't look my way, but she paused and kissed her teeth before continuing. "I'm not feeling your energy. You walked in here with messiness all up and through your spirit. This is my place of business. I need to make sure this room stays intact."

Grace scoffed. "Girl, bye. He doesn't need protection from me. I'm harmless. And if he did, what can you do to stop me?"

Khaliyah remained quiet, yet observed every move Grace made. I watched Khaliyah's eyes narrow. Her nose flared at the sound of Grace's voice.

"What do you want? Why are you here?" I asked to get this over with.

Grace leaned back in her chair and crossed her arms over her chest. "I haven't seen you in years. Not since you buried my sister. My other half. How about asking how *I'm* doing? Is everything okay with *me*? You weren't the only one who lost Mercy. She was my blood. My sister. My *twin*. Did that mean anything to you? She loved us. All you did was reject us. Then you ran with the only piece of my sister left on earth and forgot us like we were nothing."

I took several breaths as she spoke, remembering the scripture I started this meeting with. For every statement she made, I had a rebuttal, but I kept it inside. We weren't here to argue, as Khaliyah reminded me in the car earlier.

August didn't get the memo. "Are you insane?"

"Excuse me?" Grace seemed offended.

Auggie rested her hands on the table. "Girl! You've got some nerve. You must be high out of your mind if you think we have sympathy for your conniving ass. *We* planned the funeral and memorial for *your* twin. Did you or her mother show up? Nope. We reached out to you several times before Airen moved. *You* ignored *him* because he stopped fronting you money even though you had a huge payout for life insurance."

Grace's eyes bugged.

"Yeah," August confirmed. "Don't come in here acting like you were discarded. You and your mother were the ones who walked away since you weren't being paid anymore. We're not stupid, Grace. You are a user of both people and other things. Airen is no longer on the money menu. So, like my brother asked before, what do you want?"

Grace stared at me for a few moments before opening her mouth to respond. "We were hurting. We may not have shown it the way you liked, but we are *still* hurting. You will never understand the bond we had. My sister is gone. All we want is to see her daughter. My niece. Is she even aware that we exist?"

"Nope. Why would she be?" I asked, feeling my heart rate increase the longer I had to be in her presence. Part of me felt guilty for walking away without a word. My attempts failed when we were there in the months after Mercy's death. I stopped trying and left.

"Because we are her blood!" Grace slapped the table.

"I am my daughter's protector. You didn't care about Ariyah when Mercy was alive, so why would I introduce the idea of you if you were never going to be a part of her life? That was not a choice I made for you. You and Lynne had plenty of opportunities to see her."

"Yeah, like at the hospital when she was born," August mumbled.

Grace groaned. "Get over it. We were in Vegas."

August came back with a quickness. "Which was a short-ass flight back! You didn't want to see her. You made it clear through your actions. You met your niece when she was six months old. You've missed her birthdays, missed holidays, and never bothered to even send a gift or a damn card. Stop the bullshit. Did the insurance money run out? Is that why you're really here? You don't need to be around my niece. She's doing well with the family she has."

I thought this was supposed to be between Grace and me. I rolled my eyes at those two going back and forth. They did the same things years ago.

"This is ridiculous. I didn't come here for this." Grace grabbed her bag from the chair.

"Do you have someone following them?" August blurted as Grace got up.

"What?" Grace's grimace was a duplicate image of Mercy's whenever anyone called her out.

"You called Khaliyah by first and last name. I heard you through the door. How did you find us?"

"Ain't nobody looking for you," Grace said loud as hell. "I found my niece through a private investigator." Her eyes landed on me. "I remembered your uncle's wife was from Texas. When we found out all of you had moved, we assumed it'd be somewhere in Texas."

"Mmm. When did you start looking? It's been a few years, boo. His pockets are not available to you," August made clear once again.

"Ugh, shut up." Grace glanced my way. "You should advise your pit bull to stand down."

Before August could respond, I placed my hand on hers. "That's enough, Auggie. Where's Lynne now? Why isn't she here?"

Grace shrugged and swayed her neck. "Rejection. You dropped us like we were nothing. My mother doesn't want to see you. However, Ariyah has been on our hearts lately. We wanted to spend time with her."

I laughed out loud. "And you think I'm just going to hand her over?" I asked, knowing damn well the answer wasn't a mystery. "Wherever she goes, I go."

"You let *her* take her." Grace pointed at Khaliyah. "She ain't been around that long, according to my P.I. Aren't y'all related, anyway?"

Khaliyah laughed, but she let me talk. I noticed her foot shaking under the table the entire time. "Grace, I can understand why you both want to see Ariyah." August sucked her teeth and rolled her eyes. I continued, "That is something we'd have to work toward. To answer your first question, I trust Khaliyah. I do *not* trust you. We need time to get there."

"You don't trust *me*? With my own niece? What did I ever do to—"

"Bitch!" August raised her hand. "I'm sorry. I shouldn't have said that, but didn't you try to get Airen arrested for foul play? You accused him of Mercy's death. Why the fuck would any of us trust you?"

I closed my eyes and wished to rewind and erase the last minute. I felt Khaliyah's eyes on me. I'd omitted that part. I also no longer held it against Grace. People grieved differently. I figured they wanted someone to blame other than themselves. Grace introduced her sister to her little "party favors," which slowly turned into addiction. She wasn't the type of person to take accountability, and I understood the stupidity behind the accusation. That was after a lot of time with God.

Khaliyah nodded in a way that let me know I'd hear about this later. Right now, she remained supportive.

Grace's eyes avoided ours. She didn't look at me until she spoke again. "I'm sorry for that. I was angry with everyone."

August mumbled, "You should have been angry with yourself." Grace didn't react, so she probably didn't hear her.

"I will admit I was wrong." Grace cleared her throat. "Let us know what we need to do to make this right. We've settled in Dallas and would love it if Ariyah could spend time with us there whenever you're ready. But in the meantime, do you think we can have an introduction so she'd know we exist?"

"I'll think about it, Grace. This is not an easy ask. I have to ease her into this. If you can be patient, then I believe we can get there."

Grace smiled. The same smile Mercy would wear on her face. They had slight differences, like Grace's darker lips and slimmer frame. Although Mercy had her beat the last time I saw her breathing.

Part of me sensed there was more to Grace's story, but I also wanted to give them the benefit of the doubt. Grace was right; they lost Mercy, too. After believing that they didn't care about us outside of Mercy, I thought it was okay to leave without warning. In my mind, Ariyah didn't need them.

Now, I wasn't so sure.

THIRTEEN

Khaliyah

Christian asked the kids to spend a week with him, and I agreed. There were many things I had to let go of to even deal with my ex-husband. My children being around a woman I didn't know was one of them. I did so with the assumption that he'd still protect them no matter what. It'd worked for us for months.

When they were on their way back home, Ashtyn texted me with a "Don't be mad" start. I immediately ignored the warning. What followed had me heated and waiting for Christian to walk through my door. He wasn't the type who would drop the kids off in the driveway. He'd come in, and today I needed to lay my eyes on him to say what needed to be said.

"Lord, I won't lose it. I want to have a simple conversation with this man. Please help me turn my anger into love and patience. In Jesus' name, Amen." The moment I finished my prayer, my front door opened.

Ashtyn's eyes met mine as his shoulders dropped. I promised I wouldn't succumb to my emotions. At least, I didn't plan on it. I also couldn't control what would come out of their father's mouth. My son pressed his lips together and acted accordingly. After I greeted my babies, Ashtyn took them upstairs to unpack. Thank goodness they listened to their big brother the first time around.

Christian stood in the kitchen with me and watched them

go up the stairs. Once his eyes came down to me, I asked, "How did everything go?"

He nodded. "Good. Everything will take some time to get used to, but I think spending more than a couple of days at a time will help, so thank you for that."

I sat on the barstool and leaned in a bit for something to hold me up and keep me at a safe distance as I started, "So, what happened about the photoshoot?"

Christian's face tightened, realizing someone snitched on him. "Lemme guess, Ashtyn told you."

"It matters not who told me. You didn't. We discussed this, Christian. I keep trying to extend kindness and even trust, yet you continue to ignore my wishes."

"Over a photoshoot? It's not that serious. I want to take pictures as a family. They are my kids, too. We didn't take them anyway, so I don't understand why you're doing all this."

I gripped the edge of the island. "Let's break it down so you can understand. You want to take a happy family photo with a woman whose first encounter with your children's mother was disrespectful as hell. You never asked them if they wanted to take the stupid pictures." Christian sucked his teeth. I ignored that and continued, "I did. After you asked me the first time. None of them was comfortable with it. Not even Aubrey. If they had been, I would've come to you and changed my mind. Yet you blindsided them and tried to do it anyway."

"And my son refused to cooperate, meaning Aydyn and Aubrey followed his lead. Can you imagine how that made me look? My kid telling me what's what, like I'm not the fucking adult! How am I supposed to be an authority figure, *their father,* when you keep stripping away my rights to demand anything from them? The only reason he felt he could tell me no is because you told him he could. I shouldn't have to ask you or my kid to do something so small. I'm their father, but everything has to be approved by you first."

"I never stripped your rights. Let's be clear. You gave them up. The way you handled this shit was so ass-backwards. Then you expect everyone to be on board. I'm sorry the boys don't respect you. That's your fault. My word carries more weight because of the equity I've invested in my relationships with my children. The way they feel matters to me. You don't show the same regard, so obviously, they will view you as someone who doesn't care. It was like that when we all lived together."

"Your way is not the only way, Khaliyah."

"I understand that. What you need to recognize is my consideration of how my actions will affect my kids. They don't dictate my life or choices, but they are a major factor in certain decisions I make. That's where we differ. You consider no one but yourself. Open your eyes. It will help you with your kids."

"How do I not consider them? All the money I pay you to help take care of them isn't considering them? Letting Ashtyn ruin all of my plans because you allow him to disrespect me, and then not punishing him for it wasn't considering him?"

"Have you ever asked him why? The disconnect has gone on for so long. You never attempted to understand what caused the change in him toward you?"

"No! It's obviously you! I'm sure you tell them whatever scenario that makes you look like the victim. I'm the big bad wolf since I divorced you."

"And that's it right there. You assume I give a shit about the narrative. I am honest with Ashtyn. He is a young man with questions. He's not concerned about optics. We talk openly and honestly. For your information, I don't bash you. I try to help him come to terms with the perception of your actions."

"What actions? I ain't do shit," he yelled while his hands flew to his chest.

"Christian, you brought another woman into their lives abruptly. You don't sit down and talk with them to at least brace them for the blow. You just drop bombs and expect them to be okay with the devastating aftermath as if they aren't human."

"Come on, Khaliyah. They never gave her or me a chance. They go off of how you feel, not reality. Kaitlyn didn't do anything to them. Yet somehow, they want nothing to do with her."

"They do not know the woman you keep trying to force on them. They will remember you for how you handle them. Not your money, not the way you think you are giving love. They see your actions, how they made them feel, and what you do after you know how they feel. You keep brushing it off as if it doesn't matter. Then you want to get mad when they see you in a different light. Your sons are teenagers. They are young men, Christian! You are setting a poor example, but that can change. If you want it to."

"So, Airen is a better example?" His voice rose.

"Hell, yes! He is a man of his word and listens to them. He doesn't force his wants or beliefs. He gets on their level and sees things from their point of view. It's the opposite of what they've seen from you. It's why they are closer to him than you."

"Y'all don't even know the man! His wife killed herself to get away from him." There he went, talking out the side of his neck. After seeing that his words had no effect, he rolled his eyes. "You don't even care what type of man he is. Talking about you don't care about money, yet you jump on the first rich dick made available with no concern for who he is."

"Yeah, nah. We're not solving this tonight. Let me know when you are ready to be an adult. Your sons are ready to see it. Don't come back here until you grow up. You can call them all you want. If they answer is up to them. Goodnight."

"How you gone te—"

"I said goodnight," I somewhat yelled. "Get out." The front door opened as soon as I said it.

Christian chewed on his bottom lip and nodded his head once he saw Ariyah and Airen walk through the door. I realized I must've been louder than I thought when Airen asked, "Y'all good in here?" He trained his eyes on Christian.

My kids came rushing down the stairs as soon as they heard Airen's voice. Moreso, for the food he had in his hands. We'd planned a last-minute family night. Christian would've been long gone, but I wanted to set things straight. I hated when those two were in the same room. Airen always looked like he was ready to strangle Christian, and Christian always had a smug expression as if he knew the man more than we did.

"I'm good, babe. He's leaving," I told him.

"You don't have to lie, Kay. I heard you yelling." He set the bags on the kitchen counter.

Ashtyn pressed his lips to the side when he grabbed a bag to remove containers. "It was my fault, Airen. I told Mom something that made her mad at our dad."

"Oh, yeah?" Aiden looked at me with that "why you gotta lie" face.

I assured him, "It's nothing we'll solve today." I faced the boys and Aubrey. "Kids, tell your father goodbye so we can eat."

Aubrey hugged and kissed Christian. Aydyn dapped him up. Ashtyn told him goodnight. Christian finally left, and we moved on for the time being.

FOURTEEN

Airen

Khaliyah wasn't slick. She for damn sure lacked the skill to hide her emotions. As much as she tried to play it off, I wasn't about to brush this under the rug. Because I wasn't cool with Christian, he left without a word from me. Because I loved this family, we'd need to hash out what I walked into.

The plan was to eat and discuss where we wanted to go for a family vacation next month. Before we could do that, we all had to be on the same page. I hadn't put a ring on Khaliyah's finger yet. Our family wasn't official, but their lives mattered too much to me to ignore the elephant in the room, even if I had nothing to do with putting it there.

While we ate, Ashtyn explained that their week with their dad started rocky because of Father's Day. Khaliyah made sure the kids got Christian something before they left. Their father was upset that Ashtyn didn't sign the card. He also caught him talking to me that afternoon. Christian took it the wrong way, seeing his son willingly wish another man a Happy Father's Day and barely acknowledging him in that manner.

I explained to the kids how that could definitely hurt a man's feelings. No matter what happened in the past, as young people of faith, I expected better from them. Sometimes you have to do things you didn't want to do to put a smile on another person's face. Although Ashtyn believed his father didn't deserve it, he was still his father. I was fortunate that he listened and agreed to a private conversation with me later.

Aydyn wasn't a fan of spending so much time with their stepmother. "It wouldn't be so bad if we were comfortable with her. He kept leaving us with her. We don't know her like that. It's weird."

Aubrey gave her opinion, adding, "Miss Katie let me help make cupcakes for Daddy. It was fun decorating with icing. I didn't like how they tasted."

"I'm glad it wasn't all bad," Khaliyah told her. I caught her attempt to hide her disdain. She still harbored ill feelings toward the woman, which made sense given how they had met. Khaliyah blamed Christian for not clearing the air from back then to now. "At least you got to visit your aunt, cousins, and grandparents. I'm sure they miss you."

The kids began explaining the two nights they had spent with their grandparents. Apparently, Christian's mother had a lot of questions about my relationship with Khaliyah, asking if we spoke ill of their father. Khaliyah wasn't surprised, but I was.

The Lukes were not ashamed of not protecting the youngest members of their family emotionally. We can't shield them from everything, but they could try harder. Their grandmother could've at least been more subtle. The boys claimed their grandfather seemed happier to spend time with them rather than trying to get information.

After dinner, we cleaned the table together. Ashtyn and I took the trash out. I told Khaliyah we'd be a minute. I motioned for him to sit on the front porch's bench.

"What's up?" he asked me.

I leaned against the post. "So, I don't want you to feel like I was coming down on you in there. But I want you to understand that you have a unique opportunity to show up for your dad." His demeanor completely shifted. I expected this to be a hard sell. "Hear me out. I'm not coming in with a complete picture of all you've experienced with your dad. However, there's a chance for you to lead by example."

"Lead who? Aydyn and Aubrey don't have to copy everything I do." Ashtyn's head lowered while he twiddled his fingers.

I sat next to him. "I'm actually talking about leading with your dad."

Ashtyn opened his arms before dropping them at his sides. "He's the adult!"

"In some ways, people may be adults by age but aren't actually grown-ups in their mentality. Adults can still be immature. We are human. We can be sensitive and not as understanding when we're hurting. I think your dad is hurting. Especially after our conversation last Sunday."

"But I called Mom to check on her. You *happened* to be there too. He walked in at the exact moment I was speaking with you. It wasn't like I was trying to hurt him."

"Did you apologize after you realized it bothered him?"

Ashtyn sucked his teeth. "Man..."

"Listen, I get it. I really do. However, as men, we have to represent what we want to see. You have your struggles with your dad. Consider this an opportunity for you to show some grace and compassion. The same grace God gives you and me every day."

Ashtyn rubbed his hands over his head. "You and Ma really belong together."

I burst out laughing. "Why do you say that?"

"Because she tells me the same thing all the time. It's so hard to do, though."

"Trust me, we know how hard it is. Sometimes, it seems

impossible and unfair." I patted him on the back. "I get that. Try pushing yourself to do it. Eventually, it will become easier."

"How? I don't want to talk to him like that."

"Start with a text. Hell, an emoji."

He shrugged harshly. "What's the point, Airen? He doesn't care."

"The point has more to do with you than him, Ashtyn. You do your part. If he doesn't shift or change, then that's on him. Don't become bitter behind it."

"Seriously, what's the point? He is who he is. Ma also says, 'When someone shows you who they are, believe them.'"

"True. Now show your dad who you are." I opened my Bible app and navigated to a relevant scripture. "I'm only showing you this because I'm learning too. Read it."

He reluctantly took the phone. "Honor your father and mother. Then you will live a long, full life in the land the Lord your God is giving you." He rolled his eyes, then shrugged. "I honor my mom. I'll even honor you, but he doesn't care like you say he does."

"Ash, he does. I saw the hurt in his eyes when he left. I'm not sure he knows how to deal with those feelings, so he doesn't. Be a better man despite him. Your example can help him. Trust me."

"You had to do this with your dad?"

"To be honest, I don't know who my father is."

His eyes bugged out. "What?"

"Yeah. Uncle Rochon picked up the slack all my life. I always wondered about my father. I've had some battles to fight mentally, but I've accepted love from those God used in my life instead."

"Mom doesn't know her dad either. Or her mom."

"Which is why you can make things work in some capacity

with the parents you have. Your dad is not perfect. No one is. His efforts may lack, but he's still around. You have the power to shift the dynamics in your relationship."

"I guess I can try. I don't think it will do anything, though."

"Hey, that's all I'm asking. Try one step at a time." I offered my hand, and he took it as we stood. "I've lived long enough to know you don't want the burden of not forgiving a parent. He's wrong in a lot of ways, but it could be so much worse. It doesn't excuse his past actions. Be sure to learn who he is at his core before turning your back on him if that's what you choose to do. I love you, Ash. I want the best for you."

"I hear you. I love you, too."

WE NARROWED down two options that the kids agreed on. Khaliyah and I had to check availability and activities before booking. Then we'd tell them where we would travel. The kids played upstairs to give us alone time.

Khaliyah got comfortable on the couch. I sat close enough to rest my arm on her bent knees. "So, how'd it go with Ashtyn? What did y'all talk about?"

"Christian."

She scrunched her face. "You think he heard you out?"

"I do, but I won't know until there's a change."

Khaliyah gave me the people's eyebrow. "A change?"

I explained to my future fiancée what we had talked about and hoped she would be okay with it. Ashtyn wasn't my son. Being a serious topic, I apologized for not discussing it with her first. I wasn't one-hundred percent sure she'd agree with my advice.

"Boy, are you crazy? Yes, I agree. It's all I've been trying to do for the last few years. Maybe hearing from a man he respects will help. As much as I cannot stand his father, I hate the disconnect between them."

"Good. I never want to step on toes. I will come to you first next time to make sure we're on the same page."

"I appreciate it, babe." She leaned over and laid those soft lips on mine briefly. "You're so good with them. We're blessed to have you in our lives. Thank you for caring so much."

"Babe, I can't help but care. It reminds me of the disconnect with my mother. It's a work in slow progress. I just don't want Ash to ever feel how I feel. Unc shared the same scripture with me when I used to talk bad about my absent father. It helped me more as an adult than a kid, but I tried it with Ashtyn anyway. Since me and you are both unclaimed by our fathers, we may have similar perspectives. Just wanting our kids to take advantages of opportunities we never had."

"Who you tellin'?" I remember those days full of hate and rage that my parents didn't two shits about me. I didn't share those feelings with the adults in my life at the time. Had to come to terms with it on my own and forgive them. I remember everything changing when my old pastor did a sermon on Mother's Day. So, from then on I chose to honor my biological parents by praying for them and not speaking ill of them. I hope they will forever honor the choice they made and stay away forever."

I laughed at the face she made but completely understood her point.

"When it comes to my kids, Christian still needs a lot of improvement to be a good father. That part makes this so difficult, but he is still their father. He's here. He's not ignoring his responsibility completely. After giving me full custody, I imagined we'd never deal with him again. It's what I wanted at first. Not having my biological father swayed my decision to allow him in their lives. The man definitely wants more praise than he deserves." She laughed. "The heffa he's with is another story. Over there making cupcakes with my baby."

I chuckled at her pouty face. "Aww, I bet yours tastes so much better. Don't be jealous."

"I'm not jealous. I'm waiting for my apology. Bitch gone walk in the house talking shit, and I'm supposed to get over it?"

I leaned over, now in her face. "Yeah, you are." I kissed her before back away. "Be the bigger woman. We can't teach our kids one thing and do the other. Put your grace hat on when dealing with her."

"First of all, don't be giving me them lips and lecture me in the same breath." I smiled hard, holding back my laugh since she was now in my face. Khaliyah pressed her pillow soft lips on mine, allowing them to linger there as she inhaled. Her frustrating moan came before she pulled my bottom lip into her mouth, then let the welcomed hostage of my lips go. "God, I love the lips you put on this man! I'ma be good, though. So, back to my second of all..."

I snickered at the loud ass mouth pop Khaliyah usually did whenever her point trumped someone else's. "I have been the bigger woman. I ain't popped the bitch either of the two times I've been around her."

She had me cracking up when she swung her fists, then grabbed the nearest throw pillow and demonstrated what she wanted to do to Kaitlyn. Khaliyah even kneed the damn thing a few times. "Woman, you are a trip."

Once the was done abusing the pillow, she rubbed it apologetically and fluffed it back up. She turned my way, looking all innocent. "Thank you for loving me anyway."

"Always." I kissed her nose. "Unc and I can have a man-to-man with Christian whenever you say the word."

Khaliyah quickly shook her head. "Nah. At least not yet."

"I'm here in any capacity you need me. If you ever change

your mind, I will step in on your behalf. Your sanity matters to me, too. I'm here, woman. Use me."

"I will when the time comes."

I tilted my head to the side, trying to understand the meaning behind those words. When she bit her lip, it was time to go. I had to get home to avoid starting anything.

FIFTEEN

"Okay, we'll see you when you get here," I told Karina on the other end of my line. I let Airen know she'd be coming over so he can tell the guard at the gate to let her through. "My bad, so what do you think so far?"

August and I were hosting a girls' night while Airen had the kids at my place. He wanted it to feel like a getaway of sorts. I wasn't supposed to clean up afterward, and he scheduled a chef to make us dinner later. I didn't complain one bit this time around. I'd learned to save my energy on things I had control over.

I showed August my logo designs for a few of her clients based on my notes from Khanan. I finished the foundation of her website. I needed her input on the overall look. Ashtyn helped me create mockups for the color scheme and image placements to achieve the best user experience. He was more into art than programming, so I used his talents for this project. He claimed he wanted to work with me in some capacity.

"I love it! You listened to everything I said." August's eyes were bouncing around on the screen.

"Why are you so surprised?"

"Because I paid someone a lot of money once. He challenged every idea I had. He felt this color would work better, or that flow was best. It turned out nothing like I had imagined. I trusted his expertise and went with it."

"I'm sorry to hear that, but your current site is nice if that's what y'all worked on."

"It is, but it's not *my* vision. This is! We gotta go with the second concept design. Ashtyn did his thing." She scrolled through the images. "Okay, nephew!"

I rolled my eyes. "Ashtyn wants to earn some money from me. He gets an allowance, but he's trying to impress a girl by honestly saying he works for my business."

August's mouth fell open. "Ashtyn has a crush? Who is it? You met her?"

"You remember the woman I met at the church's business networking event?" I asked since I had only mentioned her once before.

She nodded. "Yeah, the one you hired."

"Exactly. After we met for the first time, we noticed we attended the same church service. I learned that she's raising her little sister since their parents passed away. The same little sister is the girl Ashtyn has been talking my ear off about. He mentioned a girl from church who drew like he did."

"Aww, how cute!"

"Tuh! It wasn't when he connected the dots. Amanda came over for an informal interview and brought her little sister, Alyssa, with her. Girl! When Ashtyn saw her at the house, he didn't want to come downstairs."

August fell back on the couch, chuckling at my imitation of him peeking his head to see the little girl. "You lying!"

I shook my head, cheesing hard at her amusement. "Nope. He kept texting me until I made him entertain the girl while I talked with Amanda."

"Are they dating?"

My brow cocked at the notion. "Better not be. He's not old enough yet."

August turned her body toward me. "Not old enough? Khaliyah, he's fourteen!"

"Which means he has another year to go on supervised dates." My rules were not changing for the other personalities and opinions that came with my new family. I stood my ground.

"In this day and age?"

"No dating. However, he gets to hang out with Alyssa often. She comes over whenever Amanda does. They make the most of their time, watching anime and stuff. Now, Ashtyn, Aydyn, and Alyssa are working on their first manga. They have meetings in the dining room, planning it all out."

August showed all her damn teeth, smiling. "Sounds like Auntie has to show some support."

"I'm looking for some courses for them to take to help them along the way."

She picked up her phone and started clicking away. "I'll get on that too. I can reach out to people in that industry who could mentor them if possible."

"That would be perfect, Auggie!"

"Girl, I gotchu. We're family now."

The doorbell rang a minute later, and I let Karina in. Nina was in tow with her arms crossed over her chest, pouting. "My husband kicked me out of the house. He told me to come here and hang out while he takes care of the kids. So here I am," she admitted.

Karina snickered. "You must've been getting on his nerves."

Nina glared at her. "Forget you!" She laughed as they removed their shoes in the foyer. "I may have mentioned needing a break yesterday because they were all getting on my nerves. I say that all the time. It doesn't mean I want to be forced to take one. I was cleaning up."

August hugged Nina. "Girl, accept the blessing and chill

with us. Business talk is over. A chef will be here in about an hour. Maya and Ms. Angelina will stop by after dinner. I'm finna make us some cocktails."

"Yes, Lord!" Karina yelled. "We are going to need them for what I have to say."

All of our eyes widened. If Karina had news she hadn't spilled as soon as she found out, it was most likely not good. August raised her index finger and led the way to the kitchen. Airen had a bar area where she created something for us.

I opened the fridge and pulled out a fruit and cheese tray. It had a handwritten note on it from Airen.

For my hardworking wifey. One less thing for you to do.

Karina took the card from me, trying to figure out why I couldn't stop smiling. "Aww, he's so sweet!" She sighed. "Where can I get one of them? Better yet, what's up with Izak? Why haven't I been hooked up yet?"

"Eww, no! He is not hubby material," August said. If anyone had the scoop, she did.

Nina tilted her head to the side. "I saw y'all hitting it off at Airen's birthday party. I assumed you hooked yourself up."

August gasped. "You shole the hell was all in his face. Dancing and everything. I forgot about that."

"First of all," Karina started. "He was all up in *my* face. He asked *me* to dance."

I kept quiet because Airen told me about Izak asking too many questions about Karina. He wanted to protect Karina as he would his own sister, if he had one. Airen didn't think Izak was ready for what Karina had in mind.

Karina shot her eyes toward August. "Wait, why isn't hubby material? Is he a cheater?"

"No, not a cheater. Izak is only selfish, controlling, demanding, and immature as hell. That's all." She shrugged sarcastically. "You are a woman who knows what she wants and will take nothing less. You can do better."

"Damn, it's like that?" Nina asked, shocked like Karina.

"I love Izak like a brother. I've seen him in his serious relationships. He talks a good game and is very easy on the eyes. He's even charming and fun to be around, but his ways will not mesh with yours. But I won't be a hater. If you want to test things with him, tread lightly and don't lose yourself in him."

"Good looking out." Karina took the drink August handed her. "I might still be curious. I'll be careful."

Once we all had our drinks, we settled in the living room on the massive sectional that I've grown to love more than my own. I put some grapes and smoked Gouda on my small plate.

"So, what's the news, Karina?" I asked. "You sounded like it was serious on the phone."

Karina's widened eyes moved between the three of us. "Child, I'm telling you right now, I'm just the messenger."

"Oh, unh-unh. What happened?" Auggie asked.

"First, where are things with Grace? Did Airen decide what he wanted to do?" Karina directed her question toward me, and then all eyes flew my way.

"He's a bit on the fence but leaning more toward supervised visits. Airen doesn't trust Grace or her mother and still suspects they have some ulterior motive behind their trying to reconnect. He doesn't trust that they care as much as they claim."

August scoffed. "I agree with him a thousand percent." She noticed my expression. "Khaliyah, I get that you want to think more highly of them because of everything that happened. You don't know these women like we do."

"Auggie, she lost her twin! They have a deeper connection. You don't feel there's an ounce of truth in what she said? Or that they care about Ariyah at all?" I asked.

August shrugged and shook her head. "I don't. Now, what's the news?" She quickly changed gears and focused on what news Karina had come to share.

"Girl! She's doing a reality show about families of former sports stars in Dallas," Karina spat out quickly.

"What?!" I almost choked on my grape. "How you know?"

"At first, we did a background check for criminal history like you asked." Karina gestured toward me and August. "She had little on her. Small-scale possession, fraud, and scamming. Nothing violent or too serious. Something told me to look deeper. I hired a PI since you said she did the same to find Airen. Fair game. Madam PI came through."

"Shit!" August leaned back abruptly. "These people won't let the man live."

Nina straightened up in her spot. "Victor told me about them back in the day with Airen. They are definitely users. Whatever I can do to help, name it. I mean, I got my sisters. We can jump her." She said with a straight face until we all burst out laughing together. "For real. But the copper over here can't be there. Plausible deniability." She pointed at Karina.

"Premeditated. You told me your plan to do bodily harm," Karina corrected.

Nina shook her finger. "No, see, what I said was we can jump up for joy in the name of Jesus the Christ. You didn't let me get it out."

"Y'all are crazy." Karina took a sip from her glass.

We talked about Grace until the chef came. There was no

telling what all of this meant regarding them popping up suddenly. I tried to give Grace the benefit of the doubt because she lost her sister. Lynne lost her daughter. After listening to stories about them from August, I wasn't so sure anymore.

My biggest concern was breaking the news to Airen. August would look more into this new show and see what information she can find out from her connections. Certain people she's cool with didn't give her a heads up. Grace had been on her radar for some time, and others had been keeping an eye out for anything newsworthy. For this to slip through made her question her "friendships" with people in the entertainment industry.

The night became more relaxing once we left the drama behind and focused on ourselves and each other. Nina invited us to join her and her sisters for their Monday night meetups. They'd been doing it forever, and she assumed we'd enjoy crashing a few of their Mondays if we were down.

August was more excited than anyone for the invite, which made me think of Airen's wish for her to make more female friends. We loved her and were happy to invite her into our growing tribe.

SIXTEEN

Airen

Life had been moving a million miles a minute. Between the show, planning for the rec center, and family, I couldn't tell which was up some days. Who would expect everything I ever wanted to arrive at the same time? If I had, I would've prayed differently.

I was grateful for every part, but I hated being away from my family. The one I wanted more than anything. Khaliyah had been more responsible for my daughter than I had this summer.

One day, Khaliyah picked up my slack when I was home, which was only four days a week the last few weeks. I snapped because she did something I could've done myself. After she kindly put me in my place and gave us time to cool off by leaving me alone with Ariyah, I recognized my error.

Khaliyah had become a shoulder I leaned on. Another trusted person to care for my daughter. She did it all without complaint. Our connection brought about more projects for her. Luckily, she had Amanda. More work required more of her time, but I also added another kid to her plate without considering the additional mom energy Ariyah would take.

Snapping at her was not my finest moment. Neither was my daughter tearing up when she heard the two of us arguing from her room. When Khaliyah walked out, Ariyah thought it would be forever. My daughter remembered little about her mother, but she definitely recognized the absence of someone she longed for. Khaliyah had become another mother to my daughter, and I'd shut her out for a moment.

That moment lasted only a few hours, but felt like days. I couldn't apologize to Khaliyah and Ariyah enough. I needed Khaliyah in so many ways that I could never really repay her. My love, loyalty, and adoration were what I had to offer. I failed to keep that up because I was in my feelings.

The news about Grace didn't help either. I knew little about her moves except that she got on the show because of my name. It messed with me that my marriage to Mercy forever connected me to people I wanted nothing to do with after her death. I didn't want to deal with them when she was alive.

A lot was going on without enough time to process. I vented to Uncle Rochon the day after. The next thing I knew, I was on a plane with him, and then we were at his beach house in Florida.

Once we settled into our rooms, I showered and called Khaliyah. She and Aunt Maya were at my place with the kids this long weekend. Khaliyah thanked me for the flowers and my biggest gift basket to date. It had more wine and products she wanted to try. Khaliyah would always save posts on IG, which was how I knew what to get her when she let me roam through her phone.

Some time after the phone call, I must've dozed off. Unc knocked on my door so we could talk in the kitchen as he prepared dinner. Once I followed him there, I learned we weren't alone.

"Ayyy," Izak greeted me. "Sleeping negro is finally awake."

"Fuck you." I laughed. "What y'all doing here?" I hugged Victor and Nick.

"We're here for you," Victor told me as if I should've

known. "Heard you needed some brotherly love. Unc made the call; we answered."

"And always will," Nick added.

My eyes welled as I struggled to fight the quiver of my mouth. "I appreciate you. All of you for coming out like this."

"We love you, man." Izak got up and hugged me as he made his way to the fridge. He pulled out some beer. "We got your back forever."

Uncle Rochon patted my back a few times before holding me in an embrace. "I heard you, Airen. You need a refresh. You're like a son to me, nephew. I'm gonna do everything in my power to lift you up. This weekend happened because of you, but it's for all of us." He gestured to every man in the room. "We try to hold everything and go full-steam ahead like we're not human. We forbid ourselves to take breaks or have feelings. Shit goes left, but it's not supposed to get to us? No, sir. When we do that, we become a powder keg that explodes on whoever is nearby. Son, I don't want you fucking up because you won't pace yourself or at least be honest about your limitations."

"I know, Unc." I nodded before occupying a bar stool.

"Do you? You've only been at it a little while, and you're already snapping at my niece, who wants nothing more than to be in your corner."

"You did what?" Nick asked, surprised like everyone else.

I told them about the slight mishap that Khaliyah didn't deserve. I ratted on myself because I didn't like how it felt afterward. Maybe it would've been different if the look on her face hadn't burned into my memory.

I understood that we'd have bumps in the road, but this was all on me. Everyone knew me as very calm and collected. Allowing the outside world to influence my mood to the point of going off was unacceptable.

After the explanation, they understood the situation had

been resolved. The problem was I hadn't forgiven myself, even when the one I hurt had.

"Everything is well with Airen and Khaliyah. However, this weekend is about learning to forgive ourselves and not bearing the weight of the world on our shoulders. We are not Jesus. I need you men to learn how to give all of your worries to God."

"You're right, Unc." Nick placed his beer bottle down. "My wife and I are so much better at it now, but she took a lot of shit from me when I didn't understand how to unload my feelings and worries the right way. My pastor helped us in couples counseling."

"Ha!" Unc smiled. "I'm glad you said that." He picked up some sheets in front of him and handed one to each of us. "This is my plan for the weekend. Tomorrow, my pastor is coming to spend a few hours with us. We're going to have some man-to-man conversations with a man of God whom I trust."

Victor nodded as he read the paper. "Sounds good."

Unc had it all laid out. From morning prayer to each meal and activities for the next three days. We'd all head back either late Sunday night or early Monday morning. I was ready for this reset.

***

KHANAN AND TYREE arrived early Friday morning. Unc said the younger guys should learn some lessons before they reached our age. We had a good ten years on them. Since they were always around, we wanted to let them learn from our mistakes.

We shared stories about our childhoods and our outlook on manhood. The pastor Unc invited changed our view of what we saw as hindrances in our lives from our youth to the present. He broke each of us down, revealing how God had used our pain for our good. We recognized that much of what we'd gone through was so that we could help other people.

The connections in our circle had the potential to bless so many lives with our knowledge, experience, and resources. The man of God lit a fire within me, and I had to maintain it to push through every circumstance, relying on God's strength.

Friday was a day of many tears and breakthroughs. We couldn't thank Unc enough for putting this together for us. If we did nothing else, the weekend was a success. Yet, he had more in store.

Saturday was a day of being out and about. We took many pictures when people recognized us. It didn't bother me one bit. I was with my brothers. We spent time on the beach and hung out at Unc's go-to lounge. He reserved Aunt Maya's favorite booth. She stayed on his mind. That was the level of love I felt with Khaliyah. I wanted to be the best version of myself for her and our children. It also meant accepting my imperfect humanity.

On Sunday, we visited the church where Unc's pastor preached as the guest speaker. No one approached us at all. The church members treated us like everybody else. Same as Khaliyah's church. That was the best part. Being able to worship in peace. We were simply men. It bothered me when we were recognized at churches we had visited in the past — not as visitors, but as people with public statuses.

After a catered brunch at the beach house, we chilled on the deck while Unc's meat marinated for what we'd all been looking forward to. He'd be grilling for dinner.

"Oh, man. I wanted to say I'm sorry about your old sister-in-law's show," Khanan said to me on the side. The men were talking about something else. He responded to my tightened features. "August was pretty heated when she verified it. I was in the room when she got the call."

I guess that was okay since she didn't tell him directly. "Thanks, Khanan. It's frustrating, but we'll get through it."

"For sure. I have no doubts." He took a drink. "I'm glad y'all invited us here this weekend. You men are inspirations. I hope to gain even a fraction of your success and turn around and do something as positive as you are."

"I appreciate that, man. You caught us at the right time in our lives. We weren't always so willing to open up."

"No one would fault you. You've endured more than I thought. And trust me, no one will learn any of it from me."

We clinked bottles in agreement, grateful for the confidentiality we all shared. I had a tribe of trustworthy men. No amount of money or fame would ever compare to the joy I had being where I was in life with these men.

Nick stood and raised his hand to get our attention. "Before we get on this grill and cook together, I have something important to announce." We gave him our attention as he continued. "Izak and I have talked about it for a while." Nick looked at me. "You've been coming to Arizona once a week, which is a big change for you. You've inspired us to move to Houston. We think it's best so we can be more available not only for the show but for your vision."

"What?" I asked, not wanting to make any assumptions.

Izak rested his hand on my shoulder. "We want to help you with the rec center."

"So do we," Victor said, motioning at himself, Tyree, and Khanan. "These guys are now with me and the classes I run with Byron and Zakari. Together, we want to come aboard your vision ship. Your vision is to help young athletes become more well-rounded in their options outside of the game. As they develop their talents, we can bring our expertise to help them build businesses and portfolios. The center can offer so many resources and information to benefit a multitude of people in the community."

"We got you, man. We believe in your vision and want to create this legacy with you." Nick walked over to me and shook my hand. "We can change lives with all we have to offer. That's only if you say it's okay. This is your baby."

I held my jaw to keep myself from bawling. "I don't even have the words outside of hell, yeah. I can't believe all of you want to do this."

"We've watched you at your lowest and witnessed how God has strengthened you in so many ways. We got you. We're in this together." Victor dapped me up. "I love you, man."

Unc stayed silent in his seat with a smile on his face. Once he finally opened his mouth, he had us stand together and pray.

I was ready to go home to my family and shoot for the stars in every area of my life. There was no longer a need to hold back. I had God walking with me, my brothers standing by me, and my family motivating me. There wasn't a thing I couldn't do.

SEVENTEEN

Airen

"A LOT OF MEN ISOLATE THEMSELVES. SOMETIMES it's in shame, guilt, fear, or even anger. I'm saying this all from experience. I had my brothers, but I didn't let them in for the reasons I just mentioned. I was supposed to be a leader, a provider, the strong one. Life's circumstances broke me down. I allowed myself to stay there because I believed it was where I belonged.

"My smile was genuine. Especially with my daughter, but my thoughts tore me down when the door closed behind me. It took a word from Izak, who was unaware of what I went through internally. Something that touched him at church the previous Sunday. It pushed me back into fellowship with God. I briefly forgot to lean on His grace. I honestly thought He'd left me.

"My brothers were there for me when I finally opened up. I was in a dark place. They helped me see who I was in God and as a father. My brothers are my keepers. They protected my privacy. God allowed me to settle in peace and learn to be more open and trusting. Now I am thriving. I'm in love. I have an amazing tribe. I owe it all to God and these guys. Oh, and my brother, Victor. That's my guy."

Jermaine, the host of the *Your Point Is?* podcast, nodded. "That's what's up. You hit so many nails right on the head. We become recluses as if we are supposed to hold everything together on our own." Jermaine turned to Izak and got his take on mental health in our community.

After our weekend in Florida, we returned with fresh perspectives and additional segment ideas. Our first slew of guests on our show will be people in our lives, with Unc being number one. We'd always discussed not being a show only about sports. We aimed to include fatherhood, married life, and single life. Nick's decision to move his entire family to Houston next summer was a massive leap of faith for his family. We'd definitely talk about that once it happened.

Nick spoke with the host about our vision for the show now that we were transitioning to video episodes. It was a testament to the transformation in our lives. We were all striving for something and linked our talents to create something bigger than ourselves. I knew he meant the rec center, but I hadn't announced it yet.

We had many private players willing to partner with us. Eventually, we'd host a fundraiser dinner to add to what we had so far. A group of us chose the perfect building. It had now become a tribe legacy project.

The conversation flowed well with the two hosts. We covered all the promotional points that August had coached us on for days. It was our first on-camera interview together, so she stayed on us as if being ourselves took rehearsal.

Jeremy cleared his throat while looking at his notes. I noticed Jermaine narrow his eyes at him and slightly shook his head while Izak finished answering his question.

Jeremy looked at the three of us and smiled. "I want to thank you for coming here and being so open about life and sharing what's next for you. We'll be looking out for the new content."

I locked in with him. "We appreciate you for having us."

"Oh, of course. I do have one last question for you, Airen." I nodded for him to ask away. "How do you feel about

Roland, whose wife you were allegedly linked to in the past, having your name in his mouth recently?"

We were caught off guard with that one. "I don't know what you mean." I kept my cool. August warned us about the messy aspect this nigga brought to the show. The producer assured her this wouldn't be that type of episode. The only thing he could bring up was the past. I'd let it roll off me like the man of God I tried to be every day.

Jeremy explained. "Roland's wife filed for divorce. There was speculation that she moved on with one of his former teammates. You mentioned you were in love. Is there any truth to the rumors?"

My hands tightened into fists as I recalled a scripture Khaliyah shared with me whenever she felt like she'd blow. I took a deep breath. "I know nothing about that couple. No need to ask me anything about them."

Izak's head ticked to the side. "That doesn't sound like a question to support brotherhood, my dude. Something you were so adamant about earlier."

Despite my blood boiling, I promised myself I'd keep my cool in this new phase in my life. Muthafuckas like this nigga be the ones that push the right button at the wrong time, then I'm viewed as someone I wasn't.

I raised my hand to let Izak know it was okay. "To ease the burning ears of all the messy people out there, including your goofy ass," I stated with my eyes dead on Jeremy. "I am in love with Khaliyah Luke. She's my woman, my love, and my life. I have never and never will be involved with another man's wife. Let's dead this conversation forever."

Jeremy leaned forward in his chair. "Speaking of dead, your late wife was—"

All three of us hopped to our feet. This nigga was ready to be in a hospital bed. Izak spoke before I could. "I will jump across this muthafucking table if you finish that question. Let the man live in peace. Why do we keep talking about the past?"

Nick posted up, strengthening his stance. "Seriously, nigga. We're here to talk about our show and promote men in a positive light. Yet, you're using your platform to stir shit up. You a bitch for that." Nick gave me a look, and I nodded.

I patted both of their backs as a thank you, but also to tell them to stand down. My eyes roamed to each pair in the room. "Y'all be blessed or go to hell. That choice is yours. As for me and my house..." I laughed on the inside. "We gone let you make it today. Do better, Black men."

Nick kissed his teeth. "Let's go. This shit ain't worth it."

"No, the fuck it ain't," Izak agreed, and they followed me to the room's exit.

We walked out without another word, not even acknowledging the apologies and requests for us to return and finish the interview. I wanted to get home to my family.

"The fuck is wrong with people, man? You good?" Nick asked me.

I nodded with a smile. "I am. This was part of why I stayed to myself, but I understand how important it is not to let shit like this stop my progress. People are going to be who they are. As long as we handle business honorably, we good. Thanks for having my back in there."

Izak burst out laughing. "After all you said about our brotherhood, it would've been fucked up if we'd let that slide."

One of August's agents traveled with us. She was livid once we met up with her. She stayed behind after we walked out, so I assumed she had some words with the producer and hosts. We left together and headed back to the hotel. August called us as soon as we got in the truck. She discussed how the show might still air, but whatever backlash came our way, she'd handle it. From the colorful words blasting through my speaker, we had no doubt she'd do precisely what she said.

Izak ordered food to be delivered so I wouldn't have to be outside. We'd stay at the hotel until our flight home in about four hours. I called Khaliyah and told her what happened. She sounded like Izak, wanting to jump through the phone. All the women in my life would fight for me if I let them. My guys stood up for me without my asking.

Even with everything that happened, I thanked God for the feeling of completion. The world kept throwing darts, but this time around, I had the right people around me. None of it would cause any damage. Not Grace. Not Roland.

I was in good hands and looked forward to the next dart. My fight looked different in this round of life.

EIGHTEEN

AIREN'S HEAD RESTED ON MY LAP WHILE THE KIDS took off upstairs for the last hour of our family night. We were at his house since the boys wanted to explore the games his big-kid ass kept buying for himself—more like he had bought them for the boys. I didn't complain tonight since we needed alone time.

The interview the guys did aired yesterday. Airen took it well since the backlash wasn't on him, but on the host trying to start shit. We talked after I watched it, and all I could do was laugh at his one-liners. If no one else found it funny, it lightened my spirits.

Airen turned onto his back, looking up at me as I gently massaged his scalp. "Why are you so good to me?" he asked barely above a whisper.

Not really understanding the question, I responded with, "I'm sorry, what?"

He grabbed my hand from his head and brought it to his lips, softly kissing my palm. "What did I do to deserve you?"

I shrugged. "That's a question between you and God." We laughed. "You are quite the catch yourself, sir."

His pursed lips and nod of agreement tickled me. It was good to see him accept that he was a great man. I never wanted him to forget it. It was clear in how he carried himself, his calmness, and, most of all, in the perfect little girl he had raised. Our kids reflected our love. She was a significant factor in my reservations about him melting away after we met.

The way a child loved a parent revealed a great deal. The way the people in his life loved him was evidence of his heart. Genuine people don't fuck with just anybody. Aunt Maya was definitely one of those people. I quickly learned that my heart would be safe with Airen, even though I fought it in the beginning. This man staring into my eyes from my lap gave me chills.

I pushed his head a bit, so he'd get up. "What's wrong?" he asked.

"Belize," I mentioned the word we chose when the other was pushing our limit to control our temptation.

The unfair smirk on his face caused me to look away. "Have you noticed how much we say that now? It's becoming quite clear that we may need to tie the knot soon. Don't you think?"

"Boy! I don't want to get married so you can get your dick wet." His burst of laughter made me laugh too. "If we tie the knot, it will be about being ready for the commitment of forever."

"I didn't say it for the former reason, Khaliyah."

"Sure you didn't."

Airen scooted closer to me on the couch. "So, you're not ready to marry me yet?"

"I'm ready when you are."

Our premarital counselor at church mentioned that we were ready, in his opinion. We talked about our family history. Mine lacked much information about my parents. My mom left a year after I was born, and no one has seen her since. His mom left his life a few years before Mercy lost hers. I'd never been so emotionally naked with anyone before. Yet, I'd also never been safer.

Counseling equipped us with the tools to face whatever

challenges came our way as a team. That was before he mentioned my name on a popular podcast. I didn't like the attention on social media, but it didn't intimidate me either. Airen assured me he'd protect his family. I was confident that he would.

"You told August what you wanted to do about the interview requests?" Airen changed the subject.

Apparently, people were interested in meeting the woman Airen Landry proclaimed his love for. A plethora of shows approached August, wanting to sit down with both of us. Although I understood Airen's stance on discussing personal matters in the press, he still considered what I wanted. He'd do whatever I chose.

"I told her no."

"Oh, thank God," rushed from his mouth. I couldn't help laughing. "I promise we would've done it if you wanted to."

I kissed his forehead after he leaned on my shoulder. "The spotlight ain't for me. After all the DMs and friend requests, I absolutely do not want to be out there like that."

"Good. I get to have you all to myself."

"I wish I could say the same. These heffas are really out here thirsty for you."

He chuckled, knowing I was referring to the many messages about how much better they'd be for a man like Airen.

"You are the only one who can ever quench this man's thirst." Airen hooked my chin, pulling me to face him, and pressed his lips on mine. I kept yelling Belize in my head.

His tongue fought like hell for control in my mouth, and I surrendered, wrapping my arms around his neck. Airen's hands rested on my waist, then my hips, then this fool slipped his hand into my sweatpants. My dumb ass didn't stop him.

Wanna know what I did while our kids were playing upstairs?

I straddled him on the couch.

Yep.

We could get caught at any moment, yet my sense of control left the room. I rolled my hips over his lap, feeling the pain of his erection growing beneath me.

"Fuck," he dragged. "You are gonna get us in trouble, woman."

I said nothing. I bit his lip, and we started up again. After a minute, he pulled away and whispered, "There's a guest room down the hall. Lemme taste you, baby. I promise we won't take it any further. This shit is killing me."

Belize. Belize. Belize.

We shouldn't be doing this. We were grown. We promised we'd wait. We'd been so good so far.

With all the right thoughts convincing me to do the right thing, I answered the best way I knew how.

"Okay, but just this once."

Airen's eyes bugged as he stood up with my legs wrapped around his waist. "I promise we won't regret it. I will be good afterward."

I nodded as our mouths crashed into each other. I didn't care about the promise. I wanted Airen in any capacity. He took three steps before the doorbell rang.

My eyes damn near popped out of my head as I jumped off of him. You'd think someone literally caught us in the act.

"Who the fuck is that?" he asked, annoyed. "Fuck!" he whisper-yelled when he heard footsteps running down the stairs.

"Saved by the bell. Again." I patted his shoulder and went ahead of him to the door. He'd need time to situate himself in his pants. There wasn't much mystery about the man packing heavily.

I looked up to the ceiling and smiled at God. *Good looking out. We both know that wasn't stopping at anything less than all the way.*

Although I didn't pray for God to stop us, I was grateful we could keep our word.

Somewhat.

I opened the door to find Aunt Maya, Gammy, Rochon, and PopPop flashing their cameras at me.

Aunt Maya yelled, "Khaliyah, Khaliyah, how does it feel now that the whole world knows your name?"

My head dropped as the group of faux paparazzi laughed. I raised it, trying to mask my smile. "I don't like y'all."

"We love you, too," Gammy told me, before kissing my cheek. "Now, where's my grandson-in-law?" She walked past me. "Hey, my babies," she greeted the kids, who were now in the foyer.

Everyone else came inside, then Airen entered from the hallway. His gaze fell on me, and right then, I understood we had the same revelation about this interruption.

After everyone hugged the kids, PopPop gave Ashtyn a bag. "What's that?" I asked.

"He left that in my car yesterday," PopPop answered.

I rolled my eyes. After everything they brought home from their time with their great-grandfather, there was more? The bag contained more than a few things.

PopPop pointed at me. "Don't start, Khaliyah. I'm beyond grown. I can buy them whatever I want. Besides, I'm investing in his business. His and his little girlfriend's."

Ashtyn's jaw fell open. "PopPop?! You know I can't date," my son stated through his teeth.

"Lemme find out you and Alyssa are working on more than that manga. You gone end up like that dude who got turned into a donut by the blue zebra man."

The boys were almost on the floor laughing. Airen joined

in after he closed his mouth. "Ma, stop disrespecting *Demon Slayer* like that. It's Rengoku and Akaza."

"No, it's gonna be you and Alyssa. Keep playing with me." I narrowed my eyes at my firstborn. He smiled hard to stop himself from laughing.

"What's up, fam?" Airen finally got a chance to greet the couples. "To what do we owe this pop-up? I see you're getting good usage of your gate remote," he told his uncle, who presented a sly smile.

They came from dinner together. PopPop planned to drop the bag off at my house before they left for their reservation. As my grandfather explained, Gammy took too long getting ready, so they came over afterward. Maya knew we'd be here.

The six of us sat in the living room. I snuggled next to Airen, feeling centered at the pace of his heart and relaxed breathing. Since my family absolutely supported Airen, they each had much to say about the interview. Gammy repeated one of my favorite lines Airen stated at the end.

The laughter filling the room almost brought tears to my eyes. I couldn't remember a time they were this comfortable with my kids' father. This interaction was surreal.

"That's the world for you. They will kick you while you're down and try to trip you while you're up," Aunt Maya spoke on the intentions of the show's host.

"Ain't that the truth?" Gammy seconded. She folded her hands in her lap. I felt her eyes on me. "So, when are you two gonna stop beating around the bush and make things official? I want to plan a wedding. It's been so long."

"Gammy?!" I shouted.

"Oh, child, hush up. We all know y'all wanna get married. Well, at least you know you ought to," she told us.

Her daughter had to jump in. "If they aren't a match made in heaven, I don't know what is. The kids are on board. You did counseling. What are y'all waiting for?"

"Maybe to at least date for a year. It's been maybe half of that," I rebutted, knowing damn well I'd marry Airen tonight.

"Honey, timing means nothing with the gift of love you share. And as a family." Gammy raised her hand to stop my protest. "I understand not wanting to rush into it. You have all the time in the world. So, we will leave it alone. But the truth is the truth. It's written all over your faces. It's definitely all up and through your body language. We'll be here when y'all are ready. No pressure."

We quickly understood that my grandmother only said what was politically correct. As soon as she finished, she hummed the wedding song.

The family night officially ended an hour later than planned. All of us left Airen and Ariyah at the same time. While the kids were in the car, I hugged and kissed Airen for the last time tonight.

"I can't wait to marry you, Khaliyah Landry."

Trying not to blush, I pecked his lips and got in the car. I felt my days as a single woman coming to a end.

NINETEEN

Airen

"Yo, are you serious right now?" I sat back down in the chair after clicking the link August sent me.

August pulled me into her office while Khanan and Khaliyah were working in one of the smaller conference rooms at the agency. She got a good deal when she first purchased this building, but only half of it was in use. Unc was meeting with us in an hour to discuss the construction of the other half.

I entered her front door in good spirits. Khaliyah spent the night with me last night while our kids were with Gammy and PopPop—titles I could now call them. Waking up to Khaliyah was one of the most fulfilling moments of my existence. Mainly because we kept things PG, we watched movies until we fell asleep.

We got up this morning, prayed together, prepared for our meetings today, and went out for breakfast. People noticed us, spoke, and even asked a question or two, confirming if she was the woman I mentioned in that almost-botched interview. Younger people walked up to me saying, "As for me and my house..." or "Y'all be blessed or go to hell. The choice is yours." If any part of the interview went viral, I wasn't mad that was the clip.

The host got more backlash than I did. Many men reached out, saying I should've busted the dude in his mouth, but commended me on my faith walk and keeping my cool. Other messages were asking if I wanted the man jumped or hurt in some manner.

My morning fueled me for the day ahead. Ariyah called me from Gammy's phone, telling me she made biscuits from scratch with her Grandma Gammy. No one tried to correct her about the name or the relation. My family expanded right before my eyes. I cared nothing for those who were no longer a part of it.

Until now.

August sat next to me. "I'm sorry, Airen. This doesn't have to be as bad as it looks. We can clear the air with the truth."

I read the headline of the article. "Former football star Airen Landry keeping daughter away from her family?" The subtitle read, "The claimed love of his life is his cousin!"

I exhaled, pushing away all the foul words I wanted to speak into the atmosphere. The disrespectful ones that would call the one person responsible out of her name. "She really took this to the press? It's only been a few weeks. Then she wonders why I don't want her in Ariyah's life?"

"That bitch's life's mission is to fuck with yours," August claimed with undisputed certainty. "I thought we were past this shit."

"You and me both."

"What do you want me to do? People have reached out with requests for comment and interviews. Tell me how you want to proceed. Our publicist thinks you should make a statement to address it. She has one ready, but knowing you, I told her to wait."

"I'm not responding in public, Auggie! I need to talk to her in person."

"On it." She snatched her phone from the table. "You want to go to her?"

"Yeah. I can meet up with them in Dallas."

"I'm coming with you."

"Absolutely not. Your hot-head ass will probably start swinging. I cannot have that."

"Ugh, fine. You can't go alone, though."

There was a knock at the office door. "Come in," August called out.

"Whaddup, my people!" Unc came in with hugs and coffee. "Maya insisted I make you both try her new favorite coffee shop."

"Lemme guess, black-owned?" I inquired.

"You know it!" He handed us each a cup. "Y'all ready to get to it?"

"First of all, this is too good!" August raved about her three sips. "Second, I need your schedule so you can go with Airen to Dallas."

"Dallas?" Unc was about to say something else until I showed him my phone. "No, they didn't."

August rested her free hand on her hip. "It appears they did. Your nephew thinks he's going there to talk with them alone."

"Hell naw to the naw, naw, naw. I will come with Maya. If it's just us men, they might try to flip the script. Something in me doesn't trust them one bit. We will need a woman with us."

"I can go," August insisted.

"So they'd really have a story to tell when you use your hands instead of your words?" Uncle Rochon told her about herself. At least I wasn't the only one.

"Why y'all keep acting like I don't know how to control my anger?"

I looked at Unc right as he turned my way. We couldn't stop laughing at the defeat all over August's face.

"Whatever, Uncle Rochon." She gave up. "Let me know when y'all are free. I will find a neutral place for a meet up."

"Good!" Unc headed to the door. "Now, let's get down to business. Show me the unfinished area. We can see what we can do."

WE'D BEEN GOING BACK and forth for almost ten minutes. Aunt Maya kept checking Lynne every time she spat out a lie. As much as Khaliyah wanted to support me in this, I was grateful to be here with someone who was there and remembered everything. Unc couldn't make it within the time we needed to get this over with.

I was also irritated because these two days in Dallas took me away from family time this week. I didn't lessen my schedule since we had a vacation coming up. I had to make sure I finished everything first.

"I can't trust you. Look at how you handled this! I told you to give me some time. Instead, you ran your mouth to the highest bidder as usual. That's not what I want in my daughter's life. A decision I get to make as her father."

"She's my daughter's only child, Airen. You didn't create her by yourself. How dare you keep her away from *me*? That's *my* grandbaby!"

Maya gently rested her hand on the table between us and them. "Lynne, no one is saying she isn't. As grandparents, we have to respect the wishes of the actual parents. Grace took a private family matter to the streets, only to paint Airen in a negative light. Let's be real about that. How would you react if you were in his shoes?" Maya asked.

"With compassion!" Lynne yelled. "Grace felt the only way to get the ball moving was to reveal Airen's true character, and it worked."

"True character?" I jerked back. That piece of shit article

did nothing but expound on past bullshit and present lies conjured up by busy imaginations.

Grace huffed. "We saw your little interview, playing like you're some saved good guy who's all about family and peace. Yet, you leave us out of the equation."

"I was protecting Mercy's name even then." I directed toward Lynne. "Why do you keep acting like I'm the villain in your life's story? I fell in love with your daughter and started a life with her. Mercy made sure you were well taken care of."

"And you stopped as soon as she died!" Grace yelled.

"Is that what all this is about?" Maya stood and leaned over the table. "You're starting mess because you want to get paid?"

"We don't need his money!" Lynne fussed.

I laughed. "All because you're about to be on a reality show using *my* name. Sounds like this is about money to me."

"Or more like a publicity stunt." Maya blurted. She tilted her head. Then her eyes widened, as if she had just figured something out. "Are you trying to use Ariyah on camera?" She folded her arms across her chest. "You already know that will never happen. That baby is not a game piece for you to use to move ahead."

"Come to think of it. Maybe you need this negative press to push a narrative. I'm the one who left y'all on your own, right? That's what this is really about. You need content and drama for your storyline," I concluded with no resolution in sight. I pulled my hand down my face. "This is a waste of time, Maya."

Maya placed her hand on my arm and nodded toward Lynne's tears. I saw the compassion in Maya's eyes as she spoke. "I don't know the angle, but it all feels very opportunistic. Tell me I'm wrong, and we might believe you. As a mother, I can only imagine the pain of losing a child. I'm trying to see this from your perspective, but you have to understand how this looks."

"And how it feels for me to have peace in my life for over three years," I added. "Then you come back in with a suitcase full of drama. Why would you lie to get attention again? Haven't you had enough?"

"I didn't lie," Grace defended. "You won't let us see her."

Fuck! Over and over, all I heard in my head was they were her family, too. As much as I didn't want to be connected to them, Ariyah was. There'd be so many questions I wasn't ready to answer. Something deep down pushed me to a choice I didn't come here to make.

I released my breath harshly. *God, why do I have to be the bigger person with these people? You know what they've done to me. How can I even trust them?*

I closed my eyes and gritted my teeth. The room stayed silent until I opened my mouth to say, "I do not want to regret this decision. You will not use my daughter to fuel your desired drama. I never want to see her on your social media. Mercy was her mother, so I will allow supervised visits to start. If you agree to my terms, we can make something happen."

"Supervised visits?" Grace griped as if I had the audacity, when in fact I had all the authority. "Why are you acting like she won't be safe with us? We're not going to hurt her."

I nodded, expecting her reaction. Grace was still predictably stubborn. "Not intentionally. Mentioning Ariyah to the public was your first step in the wrong direction."

"No!" Grace slammed her hand on the table. "I want to take her with me to a museum or park. I don't need supervision. You let your woman take her out without you. I saw them at the mall. She's the stranger. Not us. Why does she get to take my niece around, but we, her actual blood, can't?"

"You mean my cousin?"

Grace sputtered her laugh. "Again, I didn't lie. By marriage, she is your cousin."

Leaving that alone, I continued with my offer. "As per our previous conversation and your ways, I do not trust you. I can't say I ever will. While my daughter is under the age of eighteen, this is what you get. If you love her the way you say you do, take it. If not, do us all a favor and leave us the fuck alone."

Lynne sniffled. "We'll take it. I want to be in my grandbaby's life."

"Mom?" Grace's head turned to her mother.

Lynne raised her hand to her daughter. "That's enough, Grace! I said it's okay."

"Good. We can see what we can do in the coming weeks or months, however long it takes. It will be on my terms. I don't want to see anything about my child in another blog, Grace. I mean it."

Grace looked at her mother, who appeared defeated yet determined. I didn't want to hurt her, but my daughter's peace meant more to me than her pain. Mostly because I didn't buy it. I prayed I was wrong and that unresolved anger fueled my hesitation more than the discernment I might've been ignoring.

"Fine," Grace agreed through gritted teeth. "I want to meet her."

"I will let you know when. Until then, keep my name outcho mouth, Grace."

I got up from the table. Maya followed my lead. We said a brief and dry goodbye before walking out of the building.

"Jesus! That was tough," Maya admitted as we headed to the car. "I didn't think you'd go through with it."

"I don't want to. All I kept hearing was Khaliyah reminding me to give grace and to be open to meeting the new version of these women if they presented themselves to be changed. I'd never seen Lynne cry before."

"Me either. It shocked me. I hope this all works out. It'd be a shame if they mess this up."

"A shame they'd regret for the rest of their lives."

"I'm sure of it. Let's get back home."

I opened her car door and then got in on the driver's side. My heart weighed much more than before. All I wanted to do was lie in my lady's arms. I prayed this wouldn't be the one mistake that'd hurt my daughter. I didn't want to know what I'd do if that happened.

TWENTY

Airen

ARIYAH SAT AT THE KITCHEN TABLE AND WATCHED me remove the food from the bags I carried in. She requested Uncle Victor's sandwiches, so I picked up a platter. Last night we talked about what to expect today. Khaliyah suggested that I have Ariyah meet this side of her family on the phone before they met in person.

"If she sees them on camera first and talks at a safe distance, she may warm up to them sooner when they meet in person. Since you are so nervous about it, let them start their relationship over the phone. You will have more control until you're ready to relinquish a bit of it."

Her advice changed everything. We planned for a weekly call, then it became every day before bed at Ariyah's request. We made arrangements with either Khaliyah or Maya when I was out of town. Lynne would call Ariyah after dinner to talk about her day and to say goodnight. I'd never seen this soft side of Mercy's mother. She really seemed to be different.

Grace stayed off-camera most of the time. She appeared agitated at having to communicate over the phone. Her mother made her leave the room eventually. Lately, it'd only been Lynne. When I asked her about it privately, she explained that Grace wanted to be in control.

"Do you think my auntie will be mad today?" Ariyah asked while she played game on her tablet.

I stopped what I was doing and sat next to her. "Mad, how?"

She shrugged. "Auntie Grace always frowns. Aunt Maya said frowns will be stuck on your face if you do it so much. And she does it a lot, Daddy."

"I don't know if she's mad, big girl. She just wants to do things a certain way."

"I can't wait to see my grandma. I never had a grandma before." Her words shot straight through my heart. I had to get up and finish setting up the food. "Daddy?"

"Yes?" I asked reluctantly, praying to God her next question wouldn't match my imagination.

"If Granny Lynne is Mommy's mom, who is your mom? Is she in heaven?"

So much for that prayer. I cleared my throat before turning around and leaning on the counter. "My mom is alive. I haven't seen or talked to her in a very long time."

"Why come?" Ariyah lifted her head from her game. "Did she do something bad?"

More than you will ever know. "Um, we weren't being very nice to each other. So, we had to be away from each other."

"But she's your mom." *Don't remind me.* Ariyah tilted her head. "You said that people who love each other forgive each other. And everybody is supposed to love each other, even when they are mad."

"I did. Sometimes, it's hard for grown-ups to get over things. I'm sure we will one day."

"How is God gonna forgive you if you don't forgive too?"

All those Bible lessons with her at bedtime were kicking in and kicking my ass at the same time. She was right. I'd have to tackle that monster another time. I wasn't ready yet.

"You are absolutely right! Daddy forgives her for everything. Maybe one day she will forgive me, too."

"Good. I don't want God to be mad at you."

I immediately asked for forgiveness for lying to my baby's face. I hadn't fully forgiven my mother. That was another story for another book. Today, we had to deal with what was in front of us. Ariyah gasped when the doorbell rang. "It's Granny Lynne!"

At that moment, I thanked God we had followed Khaliyah's advice. This reunion was a lot easier to bear with an established relationship in place.

We walked to the door together. As soon as Ariyah laid eyes on Lynne, she ran and jumped into her arms. Lynne let out a sound that almost broke my heart. I instantly regretted leaving the way I did. On the same note, we needed the time apart. I felt terrible about her losing her daughter and grand-daughter in the same year. Even with the way things were back then, I let go of all the resentment because my daughter needed her grandmother. Lynne needed Ariyah.

All I could hear were sniffles before she finally stood and picked Ariyah up. "Oh, my goodness. You are so beautiful. You look like your mother. I love you so much."

Ariyah held onto her and kissed her cheek. "I love you too, Granny Lynne."

"You are such a sweetheart!" Lynne put her down, walked to me, and embraced me for the first time in years. "Thank you, Airen. You don't know how much this means to me. She is precious. You did a wonderful job raising her."

Ariyah hugged Grace. "I hope you feel better today, Auntie Grace." She rubbed her forehead. "You have to stop making frownie faces so you can stay pretty forever."

Grace looked confused but laughed. So, did Lynne before saying, "Lemme guess, Maya taught you that?"

"Yes, ma'am," Ariyah answered and took Lynne's hand, leading her to the kitchen.

"You're a decent man for finally letting us see my sister's

daughter. Hopefully, you will learn to trust us soon." Her brow raised as she crossed her arms over her chest.

I bit my bottom lip to keep my mouth shut. I still did not like that woman. No matter how much I tried to keep the past in the past, she still wore it in her heart, on her face, in her demeanor. She was the same. I'd be damned if she got her claws into my daughter.

AFTER HER BATH, Ariyah read a book to me. When it was time to pray, she included her newfound grandmother, with whom she had fallen in love in a month. Things weren't going to stay the same forever. I should've known that when God blessed our family with Khaliyah, there would be some unfinished business I'd need to take care of. What shocked me was my daughter adding my mother to her prayers.

"God, wherever Daddy's mommy is, please bless her and keep her safe. In Jesus' name, Amen." With a relieved smile, Ariyah reached her hands up for me to hug her before tucking her in. "I love you, Daddy. You are the bestest. Better than the restest."

I laughed. "Still not a word, but I'll take it." I kissed her forehead. "I love you more than anyone and anything in this world."

She pursed her lips and tapped her chin. "Even more than Miss Khaliyah?"

"Of course! You are my daughter. No one comes before you but God."

"Don't you want to marry her?"

"I do."

"Then will you love her more than me when you marry her?"

"No, baby girl. Those are two different types of love. I will never love anyone more than I love you."

"What if you have a baby together?"

"Little girl! Who you been talking to? Where is all this coming from?" I laughed.

Ariyah shrugged. "I don't know."

"Oh, you don't know, huh?" I tickled her until she let one out. "Eww, stinky butt."

"Excuse me." She giggled.

"Goodnight, Ariyah. My most favoritest person God ever created." I got up to leave.

"I love you, Daddy." She smiled and pursed her lips again. "But I want to be a big sister. Can you even have babies when you're so old?"

"Goodnight, Ariyah." I continued toward the door.

"Goodnight!"

When I got to my room, I sat in my armchair in the corner. Or the reading nook, as Khaliyah called it. I had to process my daughter's thoughts. Every time I closed my eyes, one person came to mind. I hadn't talked to her all day besides a few texts checking in on us when we met with Lynne and Grace. I found my phone and clicked on her contact icon.

The phone rang twice. "Hey, you!" Khaliyah answered.

"Hey, yourself. How was your day?"

"I should ask you that. Yours was a lot more eventful than my same old, same old."

"There's nothing wrong with a little mundaneness when things are all good."

"True. How'd it go? I didn't want to bother you with questions until you were ready to talk. If you aren't now, I can wait."

"I love you," I had to tell her. I heard her smiling through the phone.

"I love you, too, Airen."

For twenty minutes, we talked about the visit, Ariyah's wide range of inquiries, and her prayer. Khaliyah listened with little commentary. She let me get it all out. Talking to her was one of the most calming habits I've developed since we met. At my age and having been married before, I used to think there wouldn't be many firsts to experience anymore. This woman proved me wrong.

"I will leave the stuff about your mom alone. Your tone didn't seem eager to share that part. I am happy that Lynne is showing you a new side of herself. That is a great sign. Grace, on the other hand, can catch these hands, feet, forehead, and whatever else is needed to keep her from going off the handle with you."

"I'm sure she could."

"Trust your instincts. Your discernment, rather. Wisdom reveals what assumptions get wrong. If you want to keep things between Ariyah and Lynne, that is your choice. How was it being around them, though?"

"Different, but definitely brought back memories. A part of me is hopeful. I'll lean that way for now."

"I think that's a great idea. I'm so happy that Ariyah embraced them the way she did. That little girl is something special. Her love can change hearts. Watch. And if it doesn't, the person is stuck on stupid."

I exhaled and laughed at her always coming back to insults. If I didn't like someone, I had a feeling she wouldn't either. She took my word for it and trusted me enough to follow my lead. I prayed I could lead our family into a future neither of us knew was possible. If I veered the wrong way, I was sure she'd check me and keep me on the right path. We made a great team, and I had to make it permanent. I was ready for that lifelong contract.

TWENTY-ONE

Khaliyah

Today was a quality time day with my grandparents. Gammy chose garage sale shopping, so that's what we did early this morning. After taking the haul home, PopPop wanted to hit up the farmer's market he frequents in the summer.

As old as I was, I absolutely loved spending time with them. Whenever it was just the three of us, it reminded me of being a kid. Everyone thought I had older parents, so I went with it. Being a kid again, PopPop wanted to pay for everything.

"I see Airen is changing you for the better. I don't have to argue with you about paying anymore," PopPop slid into the booth after receiving no rebuttal from me.

"Or I'm obliging an old man. An argument might put too much strain on them old bones of yours."

"What?" Gammy said as she popped my leg.

I kept forgetting not to talk shit while within her reach, instantly regretting my choice to sit on her side. I rubbed my thigh to ease the pain. "I was just playing," I whined.

"Play with yo' mammy," she said.

"I am. Grandmammy." Popped again. I looked up at her husband. "You gone let your wife abuse me like this?"

"Your mouth. Your problem." He settled back on his side

of the booth. "You told Angelina about Ariyah's people visiting?"

I'd forgotten to share the details. Everyone was now invested in protecting Airen and Ariyah. They were genuinely concerned about the reunion after everything that had happened in the past. I explained what Airen had shared with me.

PopPop smiled. "Guess what?"

I answered, "Chicken butt." He narrowed his eyes my way. "Okay, what?"

"I already got the scoop from my favorite grandson-in-law. We talked about it a couple of days ago."

"Oh, Lord. This man thinks he's big stuff because he's buddies with a football player." Gammy rolled her eyes. "The only reason he talks to you is because he is in love with your granddaughter."

"I met him first," he defended.

"And y'all just now became buddy-buddy, so hush up," she told him.

I stayed out of it. However it happened, I was glad that Airen had another trustworthy man in his life. He told me before how it was not knowing his father. I playfully said one day we could share my father figure since we both had that issue. Looks like he took me up on it.

My grandfather was the absolute best man in my life. He was God-fearing, selfless, and kind. On top of that, he adored my grandmother. Even without my biological parents, I'd grown up understanding that I had the best of both worlds. Even though they raised me as their daughter, there was still a little spoilage going on. Aunt Maya always pointed it out when I got my way.

We finished eating and headed out to the farmer's market. At some point, we got separated. I had to check out the organic honey table. The couple behind the table explained what they offered. I was excited to take some snacks home to the kids.

"Well, hello there," a woman said behind me. I glanced back to see who she was talking to. Our eyes met. She was definitely speaking to me.

Really, God? I gotta do this right now?

"Hi, Kaitlyn. How are you?" I asked to be polite. Her face revealed she understood that fact.

The woman's head tilted a bit. "Well, to be honest. I could be a lot better."

Who the fuck cares?

"I'm sorry to hear that. I hope it works out for you." I picked up more flavored honey sticks that the kids might like to try. I showed the woman what I had so I could pay. I turned to Kaitlyn, who was still standing there as if she were waiting for me. "Well, have a great rest of your day." I prayed the pleasantries would cause her to take the hint, and she'd leave me alone.

"I will if I can have a moment of your time." My face scrunched while my back was to her. The woman I'd just given cash to snickered when she saw me. I mouthed, "Help me," then we laughed.

Facing Kaitlyn, I asked, "What do we need to talk about?"

We walked to the side for privacy. She finally answered, "Christian tells me you're giving him a hard time. Now you're using your kids to do the same."

"Whatever do you mean?" I put on my best Southern Belle accent.

"Funny." She crossed her arms. "We haven't gotten off on the right foot. But I don't understand why you are making things difficult when they could be so simple. Especially something as simple as a family photoshoot. We paid for that shoot and weren't able to take the pictures because you allow your son to disrespect my husband."

While she spoke, I prayed. I needed to listen to the words, not the tone or assumed audacity. I replayed what was the best possible intention and disregarded assumed jabs. She was not about to disrupt my peace today.

I cleared my throat to remove my first instinct to say, *Bitch, what the fuck you say to me? Then tell her about her raggedy-ass husband.* However, what came out was, "I can understand your frustration and how you think this is something simple. There is a lack of communication on your husband's part. Not to mention the lack of consideration for the kids we created. That is a conversation you should have with him. My son has every right to be honest yet respectful. If they do not want to take faux-family photos, they do not have to. And no one will force them to."

"Faux? How? We are family now."

"Ma'am, what are my kids' middle names? What are their favorite foods? Why do my sons have a problem with your husband? All questions their *family* can answer. At what point did you try to get to know them before forcing yourself on them as if they would have open arms? You need to talk with your husband about all that has happened before you, and then you'll have a better picture."

"We have. Trust! You're just bitter that he dumped you. You've been using your kids to pay him back."

"You seem like the type who'd believe that. Two things. Number one, your husband gave me full custody of our children. I was the one trying to help mend the broken bond between my sons and their father. Number two, whatever happened between me and him is dead and gone. I am not bitter at all. I am happy and at peace. He needs to mend things with his children before trying to play happy family because one thing is for sure, that's not the case. My kids come back and tell me how they feel about everything. Something you or their father never asked them."

"You need to let go of the past. I'm the woman in his life now. Y'all need to get with the program."

Can this bitch not hear? I hated talking to people who loved listening to their own voice. They heard nothing else.

"Ma'am, no one is questioning your place in his life. Nor do we care. You came in guns blazing. We have not forgotten it. If you had handled things respectfully, we'd be having a more pleasant conversation. When you lack respect and consideration in your actions, you get an entirely different reception."

"Christian loves his kids. He misses them. You just decided on your own to take them and move them three hours away. You treat him like he doesn't matter in their lives. Yet, he pays you every month to help take care of them. Your family makes him out to be this monster. I don't appreciate it now, and I definitely didn't appreciate it in the beginning. So I didn't think you deserved respect when we met."

"Who he is to you is probably nothing like the man he was in the fifteen years we were together. It's not fair of you to dismiss our experience with him. He was not a good father or a good husband. If anything, you saw how you both basically kicked me and my kids out of the home we spent all of their early childhood in. You can't stand here and act like that wasn't fucked up. You came there with the type of energy that causes people to go to jail."

"You started it."

"How Sway? You walked in and immediately showed your colors. I could've and should've handled myself better. I apologize for my temper at the time. I was in a different headspace. But you are not blameless. I wanted to fuck you up."

She laughed and nodded. I was sure she realized deep down how fucked up that was. Plus, it was intentional. "You're right. I came in with what Christian told me about you."

"Exactly. We don't know you like that and you don't know us. My kids were thrown into the situation and expected to be excited about it. everything. There should have been a slow process of learning. So, now things are how they are. A family photo? Come on now. My kids are not for show. And that is the way your husband has made them feel. If y'all talked to them, you'd find out."

"I guess you would know what's best. Your man is telling the entire world about you."

The look in her eyes seemed hopeful of getting information. We will never be that close. "I know my kids and what's best for them. I express their needs to their father and teach them to do the same. If we can all get on the same page, we'll be good. Family photos aren't happening if my kids don't want to do them. Y'all need to let that one go."

"Christian is pushing for the family photo for his new practice. I'm sure we can figure something out. I guess you don't seem as harsh as he described you. I can apologize for acting on that alone. I have noticed the rift between him and Ashtyn the most. That doesn't come out of nowhere. We should all talk about it together."

I nodded and told her, "It's much overdue. I think this can be a partnership if done right. Just don't try slick shit, and we should be okay. These are my kids. I will protect them from whomever I need to, even their father. As long as we remain respectful, we can move forward peacefully."

"I agree."

"Airen suggested to your husband that we all have a sit-down a while ago. The offer still stands. Between four adults, there is way too much misinformation. I hope y'all will consider it."

"I had no idea. Christian never mentioned it to me."

"Why am I not surprised?" I laughed alone. The look on her face was between pissed off and sad—more like disappointed. If we went through with the dinner together, I was sure she'd learn a lot.

"How about we exchange numbers?" Kaitlyn suggested. "I will make sure we find a time to meet up."

I gave her my business card. We said our goodbyes, and I found my grandparents. I told them what had happened. Gammy was proud of me because as far as she was concerned, "Kaitlyn can still catch these hands."

"That should be easy. Those hands of yours move slower these days."

Gammy swung an open hand toward the leg she had hit at the restaurant. When she missed, she had the nerve to raise her eyebrow. I moved closer to take the hit, but I offered her the other leg. She popped me twice. PopPop stood there laughing at my almost forty-year-old ass basically getting a whooping in public.

"I'm calling the cops on you," I whined.

"I'ma tell them I was defending myself from elder abuse."

My mouth dropped. "Ma'am, I have witnesses."

"I know where you live," she threatened.

"You women are something else. I can't take y'all nowhere." PopPop huffed and walked off, pretending he didn't know us. We laughed and harassed him all the way to the car.

TWENTY-TWO

Airen

KHALIYAH DID HER FIRST TEST RECORDING WITH August, Maya, and Nina. It was a comfortable set with a big push sectional and pillows. They tested out a few segments to start with. When I watched it, I instantly opposed it because my woman looked good. Like, making my ass possessive type of good. Her personality was intoxicating. I wanted her all to myself. I'd have to fuck niggas up over her. Then there'd be a different reason to get in front of the backlash. She was perfect with her loud-ass laugh and her gorgeous smile.

I understood how much she didn't want to go through with this. Because of her love for me, she gave up her comfort to protect my perceived character. You'd never tell from how comfortable she looked with the women she loved. It wouldn't surprise me if their show competed with ours one day. They were funny.

Once Nick moved here, his wife said she'd join in. Maya was the wise one. August was the wild one. Nina was the skeptical one. My baby was chill but goofy. This test episode was about the latest season of *9-1-1*. It's something we all watched, so it was relatable. Khaliyah complained about having to rewatch it since the season had ended a while ago. She was more upset about it the second time around.

My phone alerted me that someone was on my property. I opened the app and watched Khaliyah park her car in the driveway. *Why didn't she park in the garage?* I could tell from her slightly slumped shoulders that she had her reasons.

I heard my front door open right on time. We scheduled a family meeting with just the two of us. Whenever we had family plans or schedule changes, we set a time to align our availability. We added doctor appointments, family outings, and sports to a synced calendar. All this woman was missing was my last name.

Khaliyah set her things on the foyer table and came straight to me in the living room. I watched her from the moment she walked in the door. Her demeanor was off. Somebody had pissed her off. Luckily, I kept her favorite wines stocked since it looked like she needed an extra-large glass.

Once we made eye contact, she started with, "Guess who I just talked to?"

I'd usually call her out for rudely entering a room without a greeting. If she were in a good mood, I'd do it. From her face and tone, I stayed on topic. "Who? They pissed you all the way off."

"Your ex-sister-in-law." Her hands rested on her hips as she stood near the coffee table.

I rose to my feet. "You're fucking with me, right?"

"Airen, I wish the fuck I was."

"How? I thought you were at home." I grabbed her hand and pulled her onto the couch to sit with me.

Khaliyah sat on one bent knee and faced me. "I was, but I met Karina for a drink and an appetizer. We hadn't seen each other in a week because of her new job."

I nodded, remembering her telling me earlier. "At the high school, right?"

"Yeah. And that's a whole other story. But on my way to my car, Grace called my name and started talking shit."

"About what?"

"My being trusted with Ariyah. And baby, I promise you I

saw someone in the background from a distance trying to hide a camera. If she recorded me, she's gonna have more problems than she thinks."

"Okay, I will get someone on it and find out if that was the case."

Khaliyah got up and walked past me. "Thank you." She sighed after plopping down in her favorite corner. "Babe, what the hell is going on? I feel like we are always on the defensive. Like shit keeps popping up."

I moved next to her and pulled her toward me. She rested her head on my shoulder. "Hey, don't trip about the outsiders. We will handle them together as long as we remain a team and don't let anyone or anything come between us. We can face anything. Promise me we'll fight together and not against each other."

"I can't promise that. When you piss me off, you'll get it too." She couldn't even say it without a smile.

I chuckled. "Of course, we will have disagreements, but we have to promise to come back from them. We gotta understand what the root issue is and deal with it together."

Khaliyah rolled her eyes. "Ugh, you sound like the counselor."

"Good! That means I retained the tools provided. Now, are you going to use them with me or against me?"

"With you, Airen," she dragged like an annoyed teen.

"Okay then. Grace can say whatever she wants. The truth is the truth. She has no power. She knows she can't physically get to me. You are her next best option. She's trying to mess with our relationship."

"This is why I didn't want to do no damn show. If I want to pop a bitch, I really gotta consider people seeing me do it. Then it will come back on you."

"Woman, if you ever have to defend yourself, I will have your back. It's us and only us. Fuck what the world thinks.

This game hasn't changed, but the players have. I am not the same person I was before. If we gotta make headlines for your honor, then that's what we'll do."

"Aww, you'd blow up your life for me?"

I laughed at her silly baby voice. "One million percent, yes. You wouldn't put us in that position, though. You talk shit, but you can hold it together. However, if it came down to it, you and our family come first."

"Good. Now, do you have wine?"

Woman, if you only knew that I had everything you'd ever need. God made it so. He set this all up for me to regain all I'd lost. It was my turn to make sure I held onto it forever.

LYNNE AND GRACE planned to meet me at a condo I rented to keep them away from my home. I never drove straight home after we met up. Something about the situation still made these women untrustworthy—more Grace than Lynne.

Khaliyah purchased some furniture and decor to make it look like a home. If it were up to me, they'd sit on the floor. I buzzed them in downstairs and waited for the knock at the door.

When they arrived, I let them in. The smile on Lynne's face quickly dissipated. I guessed my lack of enthusiasm didn't help when I still politely greeted them. Grace wasn't initially invited, but she had to be here for what I had to say. She hadn't come since the second playdate. She didn't know how to leave the chip on her shoulder at the door.

Lynne had a bag in her hand, which she placed on the ottoman in the living room. "Where's my grandbaby?" The tone in her voice carried more suspicion than worry.

"She'll be dropped off soon." I motioned with my hand toward the sofa for both of them to take a seat. After sitting in the armchair, I continued. "We need to talk and set some things straight."

Grace rolled her eyes, forcing loud-ass air from her nostrils. God, I hated how much she looked like Mercy. I understood they were twins, but seeing her held so much pain for me in more ways than one. She opened her slightly darker lips than her sister's and said, "Lemme guess. Your woman went crying to daddy."

Lynne's head snapped toward her daughter. "What the hell are you talking about?" She rearranged herself in her spot to look Grace in the face.

Grace's shoulders fell a bit like she actually cared what her mother thought. That was news to me. Grace had always only been about Grace. Even with Mercy, Grace had to be in control. With only a few minutes between their births, Mercy fell in line and became easily influenced. I hated it, but there was no use in dwelling on it ever again. "Mom, all I did was try to have a conversation with the woman who spends so much time with my niece." She straightened her posture again to maintain her stance.

"You didn't?" Lynne asked with eyes full of shame.

Her daughter crossed her arms over her chest and swayed her neck with her answer, "Sure did. I have a right to know why. We are her blood and can only have supervised visits, yet a stranger gets to take her anywhere. How is that fair?"

"It doesn't have to be fair, Grace. It just has to be respected. I'm her father," I made very clear, but kept my volume low enough not to start an argument.

Grace threw one leg over the other, still facing her mother as her foot shook. Mercy did the same when she knew she was wrong. "Yeah, whatever."

I clasped my hands and leaned forward in the chair. "Listen, ladies. I'm not trying to be the bad guy, although that always seems to be the narrative you like to go with. My daughter is my life. So is my lady. Your popping up on her was no coincidence. I am the protector of my family. That includes Khaliyah. I'm only saying this once, Grace. Stay away from her."

Grace's arms fell to her sides before she shrugged. "Why? You're afraid she'll learn the real you?" Her eyes bore into mine. I assumed she thought she had hit a nerve.

I corrected the misconception. "She knows the real me. Not the picture you seem to have created in your mind from a disturbed place. I don't hide anything from her."

"I'm sure you don't, Mr. Perfect. We came here to see my niece, not to get lectured by you. Ain't nobody scared of you, Airen."

"I don't need you to fear me. I'm asking you to respect my privacy and the boundaries I have established."

Grace swiped her hand across the air, dismissing me.

Lynne placed her hand on her daughter's knee. "Airen, I know things haven't been the best between us, and for good reason. We've been through difficult circumstances together and separately. Losing my baby, your wife. The discord obviously caused years lost with my grandbaby. I don't want to do anything to jeopardize the progress we've made. I can understand why you may not trust us. All we can do is rebuild on a new foundation. I hope you're willing to meet us halfway."

Grace clearly didn't agree with all of her moving around in her seat. "Tuh!"

"Well, at least meet me halfway. I will abide by whatever rules or boundaries you have. I respect you for having them. I know you had to develop them after everything that has happened. I'm here to stay. I want a relationship with Ariyah. If that will take years of you tagging along, so be it. She is your daughter."

Hearing Lynne speak those words eased some of my reservations about her. Grace could kick rocks. I don't think I'd ever trust her after she ran her mouth to the press again and popped up on my lady.

I made eye contact with Lynne and told her, "I truly appreciate your understanding. Eventually, we can go to different venues and do various activities. Khaliyah even suggested inviting you on some of our extended family vacations. It will take time to get there, but I believe you will meet me halfway. I'm so sorry for the pain I've caused by not reaching out for years. I selfishly wanted to keep Ariyah safe from everyone. I can honestly say, you weren't a safe place for us."

"Airen, trust me, I'm not insane. You had every right to feel that way. I've settled things in therapy, understanding my part in it. I forgive you, and I pray you will forgive me as well. Especially after this season airs."

My ears perked up. "What do you mean?"

"I can't really say. I want you to understand that we filmed everything before we reconnected."

Grace jumped back into the conversation. "Mom, stop apologizing. You look pathetic. He was wrong. I'm tired of everyone acting like he was some damn victim."

"Grace, I'm no one's victim. We are human beings who hurt each other. Let's keep it at that. Lynne, you are more than welcome to continue seeing Ariyah after today. Grace, that choice is yours. Respect my boundaries or forfeit a relationship with my daughter. She will be fine either way." Ariyah would be better without Grace at all.

Lord, I'm trying to forgive and be nice. This woman is your child. You see her.

My phone chirped. Maya texted that they were coming up. "Ariyah is here. I guess that's all I have to say for now."

Lynne rose to her feet. "I heard every word, Airen. This is going to be good for all of us. Thank you."

I dipped my chin at her and went to meet Ariyah and

Maya in the hall. I was ready for our family trip to Florida in a few days. Maya had taken Ariyah shopping for some last-minute items, and apparently, her fly sunglasses were one of their purchases. I picked my daughter up, kissed her cheek, and we walked into the lion's den together.

Only time would tell how successful this supposed foundation would hold up.

TWENTY-THREE

Airen

"YOU ARE IN DEEP, BOY. YOU SHOWED OUT FOR YOUR woman," August gushed about the birthday party I threw this past weekend for Khaliyah's birthday. I had to go all out for my lady on any and every occasion. We celebrated her for four days straight. She deserved so much more.

Auggie called me last night to schedule a quick meeting for this morning. Apparently, she had some news to share with us, and I was the only one she could see in person. August being August, she had to get the personal stuff off her chest first. She was hella professional with everyone else. Since we were family, I let her make it. Talking about Khaliyah was a great way to get me to not care about anything else.

"She doesn't know half of it. I've been holding back. It's so hard not to give her the world all at once. I have to pace myself. We have the rest of our lives."

"Ahh! It's so exciting hearing you talk like this, Airen. I'm so happy for you. I'd better be a bridesmaid. And she'd better make me look good."

"Only Jesus can pull off that miracle."

"See, that's why I don't like yo big-head ass." August rolled her eyes and swayed her neck. "Anyway..." She clicked a button on the remote in her hand before Izak and Nick appeared on the screen. "The team and I have already gone over this twice. Numbers do not lie. Y'all are killing it."

Nick called his wife over to see the screen. She greeted us, then congratulated us on making something of ourselves now that we were washed up. Nick smacked her butt loud enough for the speakers to catch it. He took off running before she could retaliate. They must've been at a park.

We reviewed our newly set goals. August had a complete outline of each milestone to achieve before she took steps of her own to expand her business. The meeting lasted about twenty minutes before it was just the two of us again.

"Lord, what am I going to do with all three of you in Houston?" she asked. The guys were scouting areas with Aunt Maya's help. Schools and safety were Nick and his wife's top priorities. Izak wanted a condo downtown to start with. They had some time before they moved here.

"Khaliyah asked the same thing. Nick and Izak warned her to get all the time she can with me to herself."

August laughed and pursed her lips to the side. "You know damn well Nick will be at home with his wife and kids. Izak? He might actually be a bad influence."

I chuckled. "On who? Me or Matt?"

Her face scrunched up. "That's not even funny. Ooh, I don't like you."

When August first married Matt, he'd never been to a strip club and was adamant that he never cared to go. It wasn't hard to believe. He was a straight and narrow kind of dude. Simple even. He didn't go looking for trouble, which didn't explain how he ended up with August's crazy ass. Izak's first time hanging out with Matt took a turn and got him in the doghouse with his wife.

August wasn't as forgiving in the beginning. She cried for days that her perfectly innocent husband saw naked women on stage. That night, he texted me to pick him up because Izak refused to leave the club. Matt was not the type for such entertainment. Neither was I, but I'd never let Izak drive me anywhere. Matt was such an ostrich his whole life; he kept his head in the sand and didn't recognize the club name. It was a classy enough place not to have neon signs to let on what went on inside.

The way he told it had me dying on the drive back to his apartment. He was terrified of going home and couldn't lie to his wife. Matt felt so dirty. As much as Auggie loved us, she'd never trust her husband with Izak alone again.

"With all the strip clubs in Houston, I was surprised you agreed to come here with us back then."

"You were the only male friend I trusted. If you'd left us, he'd only have Izak to hang with. Hell. No."

"Man, he don't even hang with me no more. Not since he found his golf buddies."

"You hate golf. And you really didn't give him a choice since your dumbass wouldn't go out in public. You forced him to make new friends."

"Whatever," I spat, but she had a point. I never thought of it like that. "We're cool now."

"Does that mean you'll play golf with him?"

"Woman, please! I told him we can take the boys out and do something. Your husband's a dork. I don't want to hang out with him."

Auggie's jaw dropped. She was about to speak, but stopped herself. Then she looked worried. "He really is, Airen," she whispered, as if anyone would hear us in this private conference room, let alone her husband. "Hell, I don't like hanging out with him my damn self."

"That's cold. Don't do your man like that."

"That came out wrong. I meant it in reference to the things Matt likes to do now. Golf? I don't play golf. Or poker. Or go to museums all the damn time. It is not like it used to be, man."

"Again, don't do him dirty. Find something y'all like to do

together, or at least something you can tolerate for his pleasure. That man loves you. I never want to see y'all grow apart over nothing stupid. Sacrifice being bored as hell with your man. But don't let him see your boredom. Watch him light up and do whatever you want next time. Compromise, Auggie."

She rolled her eyes at least three times while I was talking. "You sound just like your damn wife. Well, soon-to-be wife."

"Because of her, I'm the happiest man on the planet. You'd better take sound advice when you hear it. Make the time and do what's necessary for the spark to remain. At least never let it be off too long where it can't be rekindled. I'm rooting for y'all. Marriage works. But you gotta do the work."

"Ugh! Golf, though?" she whined, dragging her feet toward the door.

"Seems so." I laughed. "Seems so, sports agent."

"Don't do that."

"I love you."

"Yeah, whatever. Go home, Roger!" She pushed me out the door.

I COULDN'T EVEN GET HOME before my text notifications started blowing up. It was the group chat with August, Izak, Nick, and me. August threw in ideas that must've just popped into her head. She wants us to create an interview segment for the show with up-and-coming athletes. She reiterated that some of her clients could use more publicity from a positive platform.

This woman had a whole meeting with us less than an hour ago, yet my commute was constantly interrupted by her voice notes. I guess she forgot to say a lot in person. She shared that she had picked up three new clients since the show. August thanked me for always mentioning her as the one who had this vision of the show. I often gave her credit for believing our friendship was worth showing the world. I only told the truth.

If someone made an impression on me, good or bad, it stayed with me. I used the show for the positive ones. Khaliyah's company was definitely one of the first ones I spoke of when we started. Others were businesses or restaurants around Houston that I respected. People listened, and they've had a boost in clientele and sales. I was blessed to be a blessing in the city that gave me a new start and completed my family.

Once I made it home, I ran straight to my prayer closet. My latest incoming emails confirmed details that overwhelmed me with gratitude. All of those stuffy meetings paid off. So much so that I wouldn't need to do the fundraising dinner anymore. Well, at least not anytime soon. Victor curated a list of investors who wanted to donate substantial amounts of money to a worthy cause. Those men and women were killing it in their respective industries. What they each offered blew me away. I had to share my vision with the right people to make it a reality.

Khaliyah and Khanan, with the help of Ashtyn and Alyssa, created images for my presentation that depicted the essence of what the rec center could be. I used their artwork to showcase the various talents we'd encourage within young athletes. Honestly, having teens play a role in this process sold the pitch every time. We were already incorporating the creativity of young minds to build the future.

God obliterated that first step. The money. Then he knocked the second one out of the park when Aunt Maya got me a heavenly deal on the old abandoned high school. Now it was Unc's turn. We had some work cut out for us. His company performed an inspection before we secured the place. He promised the bones were intact. It was enough to get him excited about the work we had to do.

We'd start construction at the beginning of the year. Unc had little time until then, but I contracted him for the cleanup and remodel. It'd take a year to complete. Every single time I thought about the actual timeline, I got chills.

It was a lot more space than I initially needed. So we discussed making a creatives' studio. Most services would be for the uplifting and education of athletes. Now we'd be able to provide many avenues for young people to explore. There would be room for people to teach specialized classes, study group rooms, a computer lab, etc. One side of the building would follow my original vision. The other would incorporate my family's ideas. We'd definitely pace ourselves, but the potential was worth dropping to my knees and shouting praises to God.

This was much bigger than me.

TWENTY-FOUR

Khaliyah

Airen went all out for our Florida trip. He was the yes man the entire time. Every time I looked at him sideways, he told me to chill since it was our first big family vacation. Anything they asked for, he gave them. All four of them. Because the man wouldn't tell my kids no, I made a deal with them to dial back on asking for everything they saw.

To my surprise, when I finally bought something for myself, all I found in my wallet was an unrecognizable credit card with my name on it. I paid for my things and met him outside. Airen's eyes were glued to the door with his phone up like he was recording me. He had set me up. As mad as I wanted to be for him doing me like that, all I did was laugh and accept the gift.

In the time we'd spent together, I'd learned that his love wasn't transactional. Whatever he gave me was from the heart and not something to hold over my head the next time he wanted something from me. This was still unfamiliar territory. I wanted to be different this time around. I just gritted my teeth with every purchase.

His repeated phrase during the vacation was telling my kids to "Check on your mom. She looks like she's gonna combust." Or his other favorite with every stifled reaction, "Your face looks like it hurts." Then he'd cackle. As much as it should've been amazing receiving so many things, he used them to torture me. I vowed to get him back.

Besides the overspending on Airen's part, our time in Orlando and then the cruise to the Bahamas was the absolute best trip I'd ever been on. The quality time was my favorite part. Ariyah was basically one of my kids now. The boys made sure she knew it. We had some girl time while the boys did water sports with Airen. The cruise had so many activities that it seemed like work.

When we had alone time, Airen shared how Grace walked out of the "playdate" with Ariyah. Maya told me what happened after she got there. Airen's side explained why. With the way Grace felt about everything, she couldn't take being watched by two adults. I pitied her, yet everyone present back then said I was wasting empathy. No one believed Grace had raw, painful emotions behind her actions. They all claimed it was a show to hide her malicious intent. I hoped not.

What bothered Airen the most about the meeting was Lynne's apology for the show. Although he kept the thought at the back of his mind, he didn't know what to expect. As we lounged under the stars on the top deck, I promised him I'd have his back with whatever came his way. I meant that. He was my guy, my person, my future husband. We were already in this together. All we needed to do was make our vows before God and our family one day.

I was so glad to have a few days to recover at home before returning to our regular summer schedule. It took me only one day to get back to work. There were light tasks, maintenance, and troubleshooting of minor bugs. We didn't get many tickets from our clients. Amanda stayed on top of everything while I was away. Amanda texted me once after I left. Every day, I thanked God for bringing her my way.

As much as I enjoyed this summer with Airen, getting the kids back to school was even better. We were only a few weeks in and I became the soccer mom with the girls. I was more hands-on with Ariyah when Airen started traveling to Arizona again.

Airen was out of town this weekend. The guys added a new segment that required all of them to travel. He felt terrible after learning the soccer schedule clashed with his. He'd miss the first three games, so it was my job to record and take lots of pictures. As much as I loved a laid-back lifestyle, being busy wasn't the worst either.

PopPop met us at my house so we could come to the game together. The boys were at Amanda's, working on their manga with Alyssa. They attended the girls' game a few days ago, so missing today wasn't so bad. Whatever they were working on meant serious business. I let them have at it since Amanda didn't mind keeping them for a few hours.

My grandfather and I found a perfect spot on the center sideline to set up our chairs. Aubrey and Ariyah were warming up with their team. We were the only ones in our family who could make it.

"What's on your mind, PopPop? You're wearing that infamous worry face," I pointed out.

His slightly wrinkled, handsome face, half-covered with a gray beard, turned my way. When he cleared his throat and pressed his lips together, I got nervous. The only thing that stumped this man was delivering bad news.

"What's wrong?" I asked.

"Now, don't get worked up, Liyah. It's nothing too serious."

"But serious enough to have you hesitating."

"Well, it's just that..." He dropped his head into his hand. "Lord, Angelina told me not to say nothing. I will deal with her when need be." PopPop lifted his eyes to mine and admitted, "We were cleaning out the attic to find some old things to donate. I stumbled across a box of yours that had your journals in it from high school."

If my mouth had gotten any tighter, you'd think my lips were glued shut. "That's what you find hard to tell me?" I laughed. "Why you gotta be so dramatic, PopPop?" I looked over at the girls, who were up next to kick the ball into the goal. The game would start in about ten minutes.

"We read them," he admitted.

"Oooh." My eyes bugged a bit. If I remembered correctly, my entries were not the clean version. "I am sorry if you saw any unsavory language. I wrote the most when I was angry at people."

He chuckled. "Yes, you did. But it's not about that. I want to say I am sorry, Liyah. I'm sorry about your mother not being around. And the confusion in your young mind about not knowing who your father was. We should've handled things differently."

I didn't know what came over me. Tears immediately wet my cheeks. I wasn't mad or anything. The emotions attached to that time in my life flooded in. I took a deep breath. "Wow."

"Baby girl, we did our best to give you all the love we could. We knew it would never replace the desire to have your birth parents, but we loved you just as much. I am so sorry we hadn't talked to you about it more or even noticed what was obviously sadness in your heart."

I took his hand in mine. "PopPop, in my mind, you are my dad. Seriously. I love you like you're my dad. I can admit that when I was young, I was jealous of kids my age. But I promise you, you did everything right by me. I'm sorry you found those journals. You are the best man God could have ever chosen to raise me. My mother's decision was not on you or Gammy. The decision you made to love and take care of me is the choice that made the most impact.

"I won't lie and say there weren't times I didn't feel abandoned or hurt by the situation. None of those negative feelings had anything to do with you or Gammy. I love the love you've given me. It has shaped me into who I am today. You shared your life, love, faith, values, and everything else. Trust me when I say that what you sacrificed for me far outweighs what I thought I lacked at moments." I gazed in his tear-filled eyes. "Moments, PopPop. It wasn't all the time."

I wrapped my arms around my grandpa, giving him a big kiss on the cheek. "You are my first love. You are the example I tried to follow and find in a man. Didn't work the first time around, but I'm getting there. You are my dad."

PopPop wiped his eyes before tears could fall. A sadness came over me because he felt guilty for something he shouldn't have. Gammy knew better; however, he was a bit more sensitive. Especially if he thought he had unintentionally hurt someone.

"I love you." I kissed his cheek again.

He held me tighter. "I love you more."

The girls ran over to get a sip of water. Then Ariyah looked at PopPop and gave him a big hug. "Don't be sad, PopPop. We're gonna win just for you."

The laughter that came out of the man tickled me. Ariyah was such a sweetheart.

"I won't be sad. I promise." He kissed her forehead and then Aubrey's before they ran back to the field. "She definitely belongs in this family. Looks like she coulda come from you, too." He nudged me with his shoulder. "You're gonna try for another one when y'all get married?"

"Yeah, I'll have another one when you and Gammy do."

"I'll hold you to that."

"Eww, PopPop!"

He almost fell over laughing. I was happy to see him back to normal. I hated that he had found those journals. I made a mental note to take the box home and go through it when I got a chance. Journaling became more common when I got married. I only wrote in it when I was mad or sad.

Now, I do it every day to record my emotions, wins, losses, or whatever. It was a good way for me to see what I'd come through and even recognize what prayers God answered.

Lately, there had been a ton. For a while, I thought God didn't listen when I prayed. My marriage kept getting worse and worse. I assumed I'd done something terribly wrong to deserve the man I vowed my life to. I thought I was stuck. Yet, blow after blow, I changed my perspective and saw God in every single part. He'd never left me. I heard only what my heart entertained. The lies were louder than the truth. Once I learned to tune into the right things, my life changed.

TWENTY-FIVE

Airen

Aydyn and Ashtyn were in the kitchen cooking. After Khaliyah informed me that her sons were preparing dinner for the family, I was skeptical. When the boys called us to the kitchen to eat, I burst out laughing at the plates with only a sausage in a bun.

"Whoa, whoa! Don't hate until you taste," Aydyn told me. He cleared his throat. "Your plates are ready with an andouille dog, but you choose your toppings." He waved his hand over the spread, which made me take back my laugh. There was chili, shredded cheese, relish, ketchup, mustard, chopped red onions, and barbecue sauce. "You can grab whatever chips you want and then pick your drink at the end of the table."

I nodded a few times. "I stand corrected. I'm impressed."

"Oh, and if you want fries, they are in the air fryer." Ashtyn pointed at Ariyah. "You love your seasoned fries."

My daughter hugged him. "I love you more, Ashy."

Ashtyn held onto my daughter like a protective big brother. The previously rejected nickname was no longer an issue for him.

Khaliyah and I shared a look that only solidified what we imagined as our future. I was in love with this woman and her family. So was my daughter.

We enjoyed dinner more because neither of us had to

cook. Khaliyah had been busier than ever with her business, even with Amanda working for her. My three to four days in Arizona a week didn't help her load, although she had family to assist her. Khaliyah was not one to ask for help until she desperately needed it.

PopPop had a talk with me about my schedule. A conversation I dreaded but understood. After he got on me for placing more responsibility on his granddaughter without certain assurances, I understood his concern. PopPop wanted to make sure I wasn't taking advantage of Khaliyah's love and kindness. I assured him I'd make it up to her, and this was only temporary. He also gave me sound advice about the situation with Mercy's family.

Ashtyn asked to speak with me in private after we finished cleaning the kitchen. He led me upstairs to his room. It took me back to when I had posters all over my walls. His theme primarily focused on anime shows and movies. I loved how he found his thing so young. His desk almost made me jealous since I'd never had an adjustable desk for the times I didn't want to sit and work. You'd think he was a professional. I commended Khaliyah for investing in his dreams.

I sat in his gaming chair in his bedroom, which was surprisingly spacious for a kid. "What's on your mind?"

Ashtyn sat on his bed, twiddling his thumbs for a minute.

"Is something wrong?" I leaned forward. "You can trust me, Ashtyn. You can tell me anything. I'm here to help in any way I can."

"Um...how do you...um, like, how can you tell if a girl likes you?"

My breath finally released. I thought I'd have to commit murder for a second. After realizing Ashtyn wasn't in danger, it registered that he was asking *me* about girls.

I remembered his mother mentioning that Amanda's little

sister was Ashtyn's crush. Instead of letting him in on my intel, I asked, "Who's the girl?"

His shoulders dropped. "It's Alyssa."

I narrowed my eyes to sell my ignorance. He didn't need to know Khaliyah told me everything. Ashtyn confirmed without my asking, "Amanda's little sister."

I nodded. "Oh, that Alyssa." We locked eyes for a moment. "Do you like her?"

"Yeah. But I can't tell if she likes me back. We hang out a lot and work on the manga with Aydyn. Sometimes it's just the two of us."

I wasn't prepared for this conversation because I only have a six-year-old daughter. As far as Ariyah, my answer would be ready before she ever asks. "Hell no. He's not good enough." For Ashtyn, I had to remember what it was like at his age. These things were tricky. I didn't want to contribute to his feelings getting hurt if Alyssa doesn't really feel the same way about him. "Let's say she does. What does that mean for you?"

Ashtyn shrugged. "I'm not sure. Mom says I can't date until I'm fifteen, but she knows Alyssa. She might let us date."

"Date?! Whatchu know about dating?"

He shrugged again, trying to hide his smile. "Nothing really."

"Here's an easier question." I noticed he became more nervous once he started talking about Alyssa. "How do you know you like her?"

Ashtyn's eyes bugged while still trying to keep his teeth from showing. I assured him he could be honest with me and that I was once his age. Nothing he could say would surprise me. "My heart starts..." he dropped his head and laughed embarrassingly. "It always seems like it will rip through my chest. Even now, when I think about her, it almost hurts." He took a deep breath. "When I used to see her at church, it was different because I saw her once a week. After Ms. Amanda started working for Mom, we see each other a lot. When I see a notification with her name on my phone, I panic."

"I recognize that feeling. Okay, so you like her for real. What do you want to happen?"

"Sometimes I want to tell her, but then I don't. I like spending time with her and working on the manga, but she's so cool. If I don't say something..."

Remembering how my mind worked as a teen, I finished his sentence for him. "You think someone might get to her before you tell her." He nodded. I treaded lightly with my advice because Khaliyah was very clear about her dating rules. "Ask her questions that will give you more insight about where she stands."

"Like what?'

"Start with asking if she has a boyfriend. That way, you'd find out if she's even allowed to. She'll most likely tell you the truth since y'all have become friends. Based on her answer, ask her about her thoughts on you being more than a friend one day."

Ashtyn sucked in some air through his teeth. "I don't know, Airen. I don't think I can."

"I understand your hesitation. You gotta ask yourself, is Alyssa worth the temporary discomfort to get all that you hoped for on the other side of it? Or do you want to wait and see what happens? There are some things in life you have to go for. This may be one of them. Have a backup answer ready. Try to anticipate possible answers and responses."

"Is that what you did with Mom?"

"Oh, yeah. Your mom can be tough. I had to be ready for anything when I stepped to her."

"Can I ask you something about you?"

"Of course." I almost regretted how quickly I had answered. I hoped it wouldn't be too crazy.

Ashtyn's eyes lit up. "Are you going to marry my mom?"

A no-brainer. "That's the plan."

"When?" he asked with a smile and bouncing brows.

"I don't have a date yet. I'm working on something. You want to help me?"

"Really?" He wore a different smile than before. "Yes, I want to help. You're really gonna ask her?"

I couldn't help but laugh at his face. He was about as excited as I was. "I am. Keep that between us. Although I'm sure it's not a secret at this point. We've been spending a lot of time together as a family."

"I love it. You've been good for Mom. For us." He quietly clapped his hands. "I can't wait to see her face."

The joy in his demeanor over our soon-to-be official union gave me the push I needed to set things in motion. I had ideas, but I haven't run them by anyone. I'd need to recruit more help to pull this together.

TWENTY-SIX

Khaliyah

August called me yesterday to see if she could stop by my house for lunch. We'd been talking for a while about setting up my office in her building. I wasn't sure if I wanted to. I loved the location, but it wasn't necessary. She also wouldn't charge me rent. Handouts were not my thing. Airen and his people were so damn gracious that it became too much.

"Hey, girl!" she greeted me in the doorway. I hugged her before she walked in all the way. "I know you like your time to yourself. I just had to see you in person for what I have to say."

"Oh, no. What happened? Did I do something? Is it Airen?" I shot off calmly, guessing.

August laughed. "No. Well, maybe. Before you trip, it's not bad. It *does* involve Airen and you doing something."

"And we're being vague because..." I took the poke bowl she slid my way.

August chewed on the corner of her lip. "Let's sit down and eat first." She pulled a barstool out and took a seat.

"Ma'am, you need to spit it out now. The food can wait. Rip the band-aid off."

August sighed while she placed her hands on the island. "So, Grace and Lynne's show is airing soon. My team wants Airen to get ready for the backlash that will most likely come his way. Since you're basically wifey, we have a proposition that will allow you to have his back."

My head dropped to the side. There was no way this was something I'd be willing to do. "Have his back, how? Please don't make me speak to the public."

August's bottom lip disappeared into her mouth before she said, "See...the thing is, Airen doesn't want to address anything."

"He shouldn't have to. Who cares what people think? If they want to believe lies, let them. His character will dispel them over time," I argued.

"While I agree with you, lemme tell you what we want you to consider." I nodded for her to continue. "You and Karina can do a temporary segment on the guys' show. Then we'd make it a spin-off podcast talking about popular weekly TV shows. Something y'all might already do. This way, when the show comes out, you can do a recap each week. Then you can speak against the lies."

"August?!" I clasped my hands together in front of my face to say what I needed to respectfully. "You do realize that's not happening. It's not even an option. A podcast? Me?" I twirled. "Me? Khaliyah Luke. The woman who doesn't even like talking to strangers. The woman who doesn't want to be in pics on social media. The almost-other half of Airen, who hates attention more than he does. That's the woman you're asking? Child, we need Karina to put out a BOLO for your mind because you have clearly lost it."

She damn near choked on her food, trying not to laugh. This woman had to expect my answer. "Kay, please? We need you to defend him. His name. These women are gonna pull some shit. It could really fuck with our momentum on the guys' show."

"And it can come back once the truth prevails. I don't want to be seen. I like my privacy."

"I wouldn't ask you to do this if it weren't important."

"I get that, but I wasn't around back then. You were. Why can't you do it? You and Nick's wife, or even my aunt. I'm not the one."

August took a beat to ponder my suggestion. "That's not a bad idea. However, as his woman, I still think you should do it too. We can all be a part of protecting his image."

I rolled my eyes at the thought of really having Airen's back like he'd have mine. "It doesn't seem necessary, but if you and Auntie do it, I might join you. Might!"

"For real?" August's eyes bugged. She couldn't hide her smile. "I love you so much. This will help us more than you know."

"I guess."

"I will talk with Maya and see how we can do this together. I hate the camera too, but having us to combat the lies with truth will steer this in the right direction. Plus, as his lady, you can speak about who Airen is now."

We finished lunch in less than an hour before she headed out. I got more hugs than I desired. The other side of Airen's life was now trickling into mine. He was lucky I loved him as much as I did.

BY DINNER, the whole spin-off, or whatever you want to call it, was still on my mind. It was our regularly scheduled family weekend at Airen's. However, the plan changed at the last minute. The boys had permission to take one of Airen's game systems with them for the next couple of days. Our kids were off to spend the weekend with Maya and her grandchildren. Once they were gone, I told Airen everything August proposed.

Airen shook his head and opened his arms so I could join

him on the couch. "She's always tryna protect my name like people got that much power."

I nestled against his chest to listen to his heartbeat. It became a favorite pastime. "Yeah, but August has a point. I can try. If it's not for me, I won't continue."

"Thank you, baby." He lifted my head and kissed me. "You are the epitome of a helpmate. I cannot thank you enough for blessing me with being on the receiving end of your love."

"I love you. I'm here for you. If that means stripping off some comforts, you're worth it."

The smile on his face heated my entire body. The genuine, gorgeous smile of a black man was where all butterflies originated. What was better?

"Oh, I guess it's time for my surprise," he said.

My head jerked back. "What surprise? It better not be another basket."

Airen sucked his teeth as he walked away. "Stop acting like you don't like me spoiling you, woman." He was gone for less than a minute before returning with a tray. Once he sat down, I noticed a bottle of oil, two wine glasses, and my favorite dessert from Nina's mom. I'd had it at least five times since last Thanksgiving. I paid her for making it for me, yet she always gave the money to one of my kids. Nina's mom, Marilyn, made pecan pie cheesecake. It was all I ever wanted to indulge in.

Weeks ago, I mentioned craving it but promised myself I'd wait until the holidays. I had no self-control when it came to that dessert. Of course, Airen remembered and placed the special order.

"I will admit I do kind of love being spoiled," I said.

"You should. You deserve so much more. I'm trying to hold back until we share the same last name."

I rolled my eyes. "Here you go."

He laughed. "Soon enough, Kay. I promise you that."

"I still have to say yes. So, you can't be out here making those kinds of promises."

After handing me a glass of my favorite wine, he kissed me. "Like I said, soon enough."

Airen sat near my feet and raised my legs to rest on his thighs. He poured oil on his hands and went to work on my feet. I took a bite of my cheesecake and almost melted into a puddle. No one had ever pampered me before. I gave him a bite, and he shook his head at how good it was. He let me finish the rest of the slice. I placed the plate on the table and leaned back. The peace was everything.

"Can I ask you something?" he asked, interrupting my trance from the magic his hands did on my feet. The instrumental jazz in the background lulled me into a completely relaxed state.

I opened my eyes. "Anything, babe. What's up?"

"So, you know how Grace and even August are out here hiring private investigators?"

I nodded and snickered. In what world of mine did people do that? If someone didn't want to be found, we left them that way. They had their reasons.

"Do you think you ever want to find your mom?" His eyes were on me. My entire body stiffened, which he obviously noticed. Airen pulled at my foot until I was close enough for him to lift my legs and rest them on his lap. "Babe, don't shut down. I only wondered if that was something you ever thought about."

Taking a deep breath to calm my marathoning heart at the mention of my mother, or rather, the thought of meeting her. I'd concluded that she wanted nothing to do with me decades ago. My desire for her was dead and gone. In my mind, so was she.

I cleared my throat and asked him an equally annoying question. "Would you? Have you? With your mom?"

"I don't have to. Unc actually still talks to her. She *is* his little sister. He understands that our relationship is beyond help. God is working on me, but I'm not holding my breath."

"Babe, that's not true. If you wanted to mend things, I'm pretty sure she'd be open to it."

"Nah." He shook his head. "Even if she was, I couldn't trust her. She put a price tag on my personal life and cashed out. I will never allow her to do that to you or our kids."

"I hear you. However, you're considering forgiving Grace and Lynne. Why not the woman who brought you into this world?"

The pace of Airen's breathing changed. I understood it was a sensitive topic, but we were here. "Have you forgiven yours?" he inquired.

"As a matter of fact, I have. That doesn't mean she gets a pass to come in after the choice she made. She cut all ties with her family. Her sister doesn't have any contact with her. Her parents haven't heard from her since she left. That's completely different. Yours raised you, Airen." I got off him and walked to the kitchen to get some water. Also, to get some distance between us.

Why was he trying to turn this back on me like I was more wrong for not wanting anything to do with a woman who abandoned her family and child with no word of why or where she was?

Aunt Maya searched for her for years after she left. She found out which school she had graduated from. Then it was like she vanished. Her name wasn't in any criminal database or morgue. The understanding that she didn't want to be found came after the failed search. We came to terms with it and accepted it for what it was.

I filled a glass with water and leaned against the island to quench my thirst. Airen walked in. His head was low, but since he was so tall, I had to look up to meet his eyes. He took the glass from me and set it on the counter. After resting his forehead on mine, he finally spoke. "I'm sorry."

"Okay."

We broke away from each other. "This is a sore topic for both of us, baby. I promised you I'd be transparent. I had questions about your mom because of what I'd gone through with mine. You never talk about it, so I wondered how you felt. I don't want you mad at me."

"I'm not mad. It's a really fucked-up situation. I guess I'm not fully over it."

"Oh, I know. You told the therapist to move on when he kept pressing," he reminded me. I snickered at the memory of one of our many premarital sessions. One of the church elders was a therapist, along with her husband. We've had sessions with both of them together and individually. It helped us navigate so much of our past, present, and future possibilities. "We said we'd deal with those hard conversations on our own. I want to keep my word to you."

"You're right, but you shut down too. You treat it like it's the same. It's not. Your mom took advantage of you, and you cut off the relationship. I was barely one when mine made that choice for me. I was doing good until I had my babies. I couldn't imagine ever doing that to them. It's fucked up, and the thought of her puts me in a negative place."

"All the more reason to find her. Maybe you can confront these emotions, find resolution, and move on knowing you did all you could do."

"Why? She doesn't deserve that." I stared up at him, unblinking. I needed to hear his reasoning.

Airen's shoulders dropped. "Baby? Come on. She was a kid herself. You said so."

"Forty years, Airen!" I pushed my way out of his grasp. "She hasn't been that kid in a long time."

"How do you know that? Some people stay in that mindset when they make messed up choices. She may be stuck there herself."

"That's not my problem." I crossed my arms over my chest, not wanting to hear his damn logic.

"I guess that means this conversation is over," he deduced from my posture.

I slowly took steps closer to him and looked up so he'd hear me clearly. "You know what? Here's the deal. When you talk to your mother and forgive her, we will search for mine."

Airen pressed his lips together and nodded. "Okay. I guess we're taking this shit to the grave then." I burst out laughing, and so did he. "Fuck that! I can't bring her into my life so she can fuck it up again."

I wrapped my arms around his waist. "You have more power than you think. She can only do what you allow. You can keep her at arm's length like you are doing with Mercy's family."

He wrapped his arms around me and looked up at the ceiling. "Man, we both need to have some serious talks with God about that." His eyes fell on me again.

"I agree. 'Cause being abandoned by both parents never really goes away. We've just learned how to live with it. As much as I hate that you want me to face it, maybe we will one day."

"Yeah. Maybe."

TWENTY-SEVEN

Airen

As soon as we walked inside Khaliyah's house, I darted for her bedroom's bathroom. I couldn't do what I needed to do in a guest bathroom. I probably went too hard on the ice cream after eating so much junk while we bowled. I made a mental note that I might be lactose intolerant.

When I finished taking care of business, I heard two people going back and forth. I figured it wasn't the kids because none of them could whisper worth a damn. Khaliyah was definitely a participant in the conversation.

I waited at the doorway of Khaliyah's room, trying to make sense of what was being said. I recognized the male voice dropping f-bombs on my lady. With quickness, I exited the bedroom and darted toward the foyer where the two of them were.

I walked up behind Khaliyah and witnessed her ex scowl like usual since he refused to accept I wasn't going anywhere. I rested my hand on her hip. I kept my voice low. "Ay, whatever y'all are fighting about needs to stop. The kids are upstairs. The last thing they need to witness is the division between their parents. What's the problem?"

Christian sucked his teeth. "No disrespect, but you don't belong in this conversation. This is my family. I need to talk to the mother of my children."

"With all due disrespect, this is my family now. Your

DNA *is* at play, my nigga. I understand that much. But it's my job to protect them. Those boys come to me with their questions, issues, and even about you. They are very much my concern. So is the mother of your children and the future mother of mine." I rested my hand on Khaliyah's stomach. On the same petty page, she looked up at me and pursed her lips for a kiss. Then I smirked and winked. My woman placed her hand on mine. Christian's expression was worth every deceitful gesture.

I continued, "This woman will have my last name. I'm not going anywhere. At some point, we're going to have to talk and get some things straight. We can do it now or wait until after the wedding. You dropping by whenever is done. Give Khaliyah enough respect to grant permission for you to come to her home."

Christian sucked his teeth loudly enough to damn near echo in the foyer. "You won't last long. My sons only fuck with you because you played ball. You were more impressive on the field than at maintaining a healthy relationship. Otherwise, your business wouldn't have flooded my timeline years ago. It's only a matter of time before Khaliyah is the next casualty. But what you not finna do is fuck up my kids' lives in the process."

All I could do was nod and laugh. "I can see why a nigga like you would be messy enough to read bullshit and call it Bible. That's on you. The proof is in the love this family has for me. I know my lane, and I will stay in it as long as you stay in yours. As their protector, I said what I said. If you want insight into how your sons feel about you, I can give you some advice. The last thing I want is for Ashtyn to grow up hating the man who brought him into this world. I'm here to help, not hinder. You can take it or leave it."

The wince on his face revealed that I'd hit a nerve. Christian stared at Khaliyah for a few seconds before conceding. No one had anything else to say. I wasn't trying to wound the man, but he had difficulty understanding when to shut up.

With no other choice but to be the bigger person, I suggested, "It seems like an adult conversation needs to be had. How about we plan a time where you and your wife can sit down with us? We can put everything on the table and find a healthy way to move forward for the kids' sake. You guys need boundaries and schedules in place now that you live in Houston. Pop-ups ain't gonna work anymore."

Khaliyah nodded. "I agree. We can find a time and place and make it happen."

Christian swiped at the air. "Whatever. I will let you know if we can do that," he directed toward his ex-wife.

"Let's turn that if into a sure thing. It's for your children. Isn't that why you're causing a scene in the first place?" I asked him.

Christian's mouth tightened while he took steps backward. He didn't say another word before walking out the door.

Khaliyah locked the door and rushed back to embrace me. Her arms held on tightly as she rested her head on my chest. "I love you, Airen. You never cease to amaze me." She looked up at me. "I have never been loved or protected this way before. I can't even explain how much it means to me."

"Always, babe. I love you more. Ain't nobody scared of that nigga. He will have to fall in line or get hit every single time he tries to come at you crazy. If I'm here, he will have to deal with me."

"Shoot, I'm all for it."

Khaliyah led me to the couch and snuggled up against me when we sat. For a few moments, we sat in silence as I stroked her head. I thought about my proposal for the adults to have a conversation. "Do you think he will actually agree to meet with us?"

She shrugged. "The old Christian wouldn't dare. Especially since you were the one who suggested it."

"So, you think he's changed?"

"Not really. He still wants control and free rein. It's necessary, as parents, for all the adults involved to be on the same page. I hope it will happen at some point. If he keeps getting shot down, he might consider it."

"Shot down how?"

"Like me not answering the door and letting him in when he pops up. Not responding to disrespectful messages. Just not engaging with anything less than respectful."

"Let me see your text messages."

"No!"

"Woman?"

"Airen, no. It's only going to piss you off even more. We will make this work in due time. For now, let's enjoy our peace."

The moment the words came out of her mouth, the girls came running down the stairs. They wanted to have a sleepover on a school night. Khaliyah poked her lip out with the girls to convince me.

"Fine." I caved. The girls cheered. "I will be back in the morning with your backpack and lunch. I'm dropping you off at school myself. I'm sure you have a stash of clothes here," I told my daughter. Khaliyah laughed since she's the one who shared that information with me. The girls were stashing clothes at our houses for moments like these.

"Thank you, Daddy." Ariyah jumped into my arms.

"Yes! Thank you, Daddy," Aubrey repeated, hugging me as well. That shook me. Was it an accident? She probably just repeated what Ariyah said.

Khaliyah had the same shocked look on her face but said nothing. The girls took off, running back upstairs.

"You heard that, right?" I asked Khaliyah.

"I did."

"She probably said it by mistake."

"If she says it again, it was intentional. We will wait and see. I don't want to bring attention to it and make her think she'd done something wrong."

"Daddy?" I said, not able to stop smiling.

"I guess you really are making your mark in this family." Khaliyah kissed my cheek.

"Yo!" I pulled my fist to my mouth. "I'm really about to have four kids?! It's cool if they call me Airen, but man, they're gonna have my ass crying if they give me a title with that much importance."

"Airen, if you become their stepfather, they will hold you in high regard. They are missing things with their dad that they get from you. It wouldn't surprise me."

"I hear you. Yet, we need to take that 'if' out of your throat. It's when, woman. When."

Khaliyah

"Mom, we need your help," Aydyn said as he sat next to my feet on the other side of the sectional.

Ashtyn had a notebook and a pencil in his hands. "What would be your dream proposal?" He sat next to me.

"What?" I was alert after that question.

"It's for our manga." Aydyn cleared up. I made sure not to show disappointment. I almost thought Airen had told them to ask me.

Ashtyn admitted, "We don't really know how it works. You're a girl, sooooo, what would be the perfect proposal?"

I sat up all the way, and Ashtyn damn near sat on my hip trying to squeeze between me and his brother. "Boy, back up. You did not put on enough deodorant to be that close," I lied to mess with him. My baby actually smelled good. Lord knows I wanted to forget the days he didn't. We fought for a long time before he became consistent.

Aydyn burst out laughing when he knew he shouldn't have. Ashtyn called him out, "How you laughing when you smell like rotten onions?"

I failed in my attempt not to instigate by laughing and clowning Aydyn. Ashtyn definitely got that mouth from me. A pillow flew toward Ashtyn, but hit me instead. We jumped to our feet. "Oh, you done did it now," I said, grabbing a pillow and fake throwing it at Aydyn so when he ducked, I chucked it right upside his head. Since he was squatting, he lost his balance.

Ashtyn cracked up all over again and got hit right in the face with the same pillow. "It's on!" Ashtyn took a pillow and aimed at his brother. Aydyn took off running upstairs. We were right behind them. He wasn't fast enough for his big brother. The pillow hit the back of Aydyn's legs, tripping him. The way he yelped when he fell to the carpet had me on the floor.

"Pillow fight!" Aubrey yelled from out of nowhere, hitting all three of us with a quickness.

We took pillows from the game room sectional and their bedrooms. Aydyn and I were against Aubrey and Ashtyn. After ten minutes, we wore ourselves out, chilled on the floor with all the pillows, and watched an episode of *Jurassic World: Chaos Theory*.

Although it was still early, I took a long shower and got into my pajamas. With the kids busy in their own worlds upstairs, I finally reached that time of the day when I didn't have to wear the "mommy" hat. No one needed anything.

I spent most of the day cleaning since I didn't have too much work this morning. I had Amanda to thank for that. She was worth every penny. We were a team made in heaven, but if we got any more clients, we'd need a third person. With AI in the game, I thought gaining new clients would be harder. Luckily, many people preferred a person on the other end, which contributed to our success.

The moment I turned on the fan, got under the covers, and turned the TV on, the boys invaded my room to finish the conversation from earlier. They had to have some type of Mommy's-too-comfortable radar with a mission to disrupt my peace.

I gave them details of what I'd consider a perfect proposal. Then I gave them other ideas of popular trends people did nowadays. Ashtyn took notes, making me excited to see what they'd come up with in their story. I shooed them away so I could catch up on some shows.

"Wait! One more thing." Ashtyn handed me his phone. "I found this site for reference. Which ring would you pick? I have to send it to Alyssa so she can draw it."

"Any ring will be a great ring." I looked at the prices. "Damn, who is the character you got buying these expensive ass rings?"

The boys laughed. "I can't tell you. You have to wait to read it." Ashtyn winked at me.

"I guess. But this is still too much," I complained as I scrolled through these so-called sales.

Aydyn nudged me. "Mom, just pick one. Your favorite one, no matter how much it costs. We're only drawing it!"

Okay, smartass. "Fine." I scrolled for maybe five minutes and found the perfect ring. "Here." I gave Ashtyn his phone.

"You'd wear this one?" Ashtyn asked to make sure I picked something I liked. They acted like they were making it about me.

I answered honestly, "One hundred percent."

"Thanks, Ma." Ashtyn smiled with more joy than I'd seen in a while. "I'll send it now. She wanted to sketch it out today for the close-up view."

"Aww, sounds like your project is coming along." I tapped Ashtyn's knee.

"It is! I can't wait for you to see it when it's done." My firstborn cheesed away. It made me suspicious, but it may have something to do with Alyssa.

Aydyn shared, "I finished my part." He was a co-author. His strength was in writing instead of drawing. Ashtyn was talented in both areas, but he still worked with his little brother.

"I mean, being that I pushed both your colossal heads out,

I should see it throughout the process. You always show me what you're working on." I pouted to no avail.

"Not this time. We need it to be perfect," Ashtyn said.

"It will be," I assured him.

"Love you, Ma. Thank you," Ashtyn told me before running out of my room with his brother in tow.

Lord, I thank you. They could get into so many things these days. Writing and drawing. I'll take it.

TWENTY-NINE

Khaliyah

Kaitlyn texted me when she was on the way with Christian. Airen parked the car when I replied that we'd go in and get a table for the four of us. I dropped my head back, regretting the whole thing. When Airen looked at me, he sighed.

"Baby, this is important and has to happen for the sake of everyone involved."

I pouted anyway. "I know. He just gets on my damn nerves. This will not be easy for me."

"Nothing worth doing ever is." Airen grabbed my hand and kissed it.

Once he exited the car, I waited for him to come to my side and open my door. He damn near trained me not to open doors around him. What he called hard-headed was simply a habit. The only men who opened my doors were PopPop and my sons. However, car doors weren't one of them. Airen placed the responsibility on himself, and I eventually rolled with it.

Airen led the way inside. We were seated five minutes before I heard Christian. I was so glad Airen prayed while we waited for them.

"Here this nigga goes," I mumbled under my breath.

Airen squeezed my hand under the table. "Be nice, baby."

"You set me up?" Christian asked Kaitlyn.

Christian took a seat after she narrowed her eyes at him. She walked to my side and hugged me. I stiffened because no one had informed me we were on hugging terms. Airen cleared his throat with a smirk on his face. I assumed he'd noticed my discomfort during the embrace.

"You always find a way to get what you want, even when I don't agree," Christian said, staring at me. "Now, you got my woman involved. That's low."

"Actually, this was my idea," his woman admitted.

Our waitress came to get our drink order. Christian was the only one who ordered alcohol. As much as I wanted some, I'd wait until we got home so I could get through this with a clear head.

Christian gestured between me and his wife. "So y'all friends or something now?"

"We're women who are tired of the lies and want to make this a pleasant situation for all of us," I answered. "There seems to be too much miscommunication in the mix. This way, we can all be on the same page and stay in our respective lanes."

"Lanes?" Christian scoffed.

"Yep," Airen said. "Lanes, boundaries. Understanding our place and where each of us fits in concerning the children is important. Don't you think it's time? We are all here to stay. Let's work together for their sake. Get out of our egos and the past for once."

"Who are you to say anything regarding *my* kids? You aren't their father. *I* am."

"A fact you repeat whenever I'm around. With boundaries in place, you will understand my role in your and Khaliyah's children's lives," Airen clarified calmly. I turned to him and smiled.

"Y'all not married. You shouldn't even have a seat at the table." Christian played the same tired song.

Kaitlyn winced as he spoke, so I asked her what was wrong. She hesitated, then stared at Christian for a few moments. His face was telling her to keep her mouth shut about something. I recognized that look.

I thought she folded to his unspoken request, so I moved on. "Look, we—"

"We're not either," she spoke at the same time.

My eyes bounced between the couple. "Not what?"

Kaitlyn moved her right arm across her chest and rested it on her left shoulder. Her eyes stayed on mine. "We're not married. We haven't made it official."

I looked at Airen, who wore the same hiked brow and tight mouth as I did. Christian had no filter to hide behind. I didn't expect things to go this way.

Christian massaged his forehead and kept his eyes closed for a bit before whispering through his teeth, "Kaitlyn."

The waitress came back with our drinks and took our orders. Airen and I stuck with appetizers to share. We'd eat somewhere else later if we still had appetites. The young woman left us again.

Kaitlyn shrugged. "I'm tired of lying about it. Christian wanted to make it clear that he had moved on, so you wouldn't try to come back to him. He swore that you'd try to use the kids to get him. He needed me in place so you couldn't. I came in feeling like I had to make my mark fast and hard."

I burst out laughing and apologized for startling the other guests at nearby tables. "What? Boy, why would you tell that lie? After everything *you* did?" I couldn't believe it. "Your sons don't even like being around you. Why the hell would I use them to return to the one person partly responsible for the worst years of my life? You are so wrong for that."

"Worst years?" Kaitlyn asked.

"Yes! I will not air out everything that he's done to me and the family we once shared. That's between y'all now. But I'd be damned if I ran back to trauma. You are truly delusional," I told him. Christian folded his arms, resting them on the table. Airen caressed my leg. The simple gesture settled me.

"Can I ask one thing?" Kaitlyn directed toward me. I nodded. "Did he ever abuse you?"

Christian sucked his teeth. "Really?"

I ignored him. "Not physically. Emotionally? Verbally? Financially? Absolutely. I forgave him and moved on."

"Interesting." Kaitlyn took a deep breath. I assumed the story didn't add up.

"Yo, you need to stop acting like I was some horrible person. You didn't live up to what I expected of you. You didn't keep your end of the deal. Leaving a good job because of a little bullying. That was a bullshit excuse."

Airen raised his hand slightly above the table. "Watch your tone and your words. Disrespect is unnecessary." He rested his eyes on Christian, ready for a rebuttal that never came.

"One more thing," Kaitlyn spoke up again. When she knew she had my attention, she asked, "Did you cheat on him?"

"No!" I quickly answered.

"Since y'all just talked about you quitting your job, did you actually refuse to work after you had kids because you felt men were the only ones who were supposed to work?"

"You said that?" I looked at Christian. "Wow! You really rewrote the past, huh?"

For a few minutes, I explained to her what the situation was regarding my work. Why I left corporate America and created my business. I threw in a few things that her so-called husband said about those decisions. Plus, the way his parents guilt-tripped me about it whenever we were all together. I even told her about the Thanksgiving when he told me he was divorcing me in front of his family.

Christian sat there quietly, which surprised the hell out of me. He always defended his lies because his perspective was the only one that counted. Today, he had absolutely nothing to say. It was rare to be in the same room without some B.S. coming out of his mouth.

Kaitlyn nodded a few times before leaning back in her seat. The wheels seemed to turn in her mind. This was not the main reason we came here. To keep us on the right path, I asked, "So, are y'all planning to get married soon? Or do we need to have this conversation with just Christian?" I rubbed it in his face since he tried to do the same thing with Airen earlier.

Kaitlyn, surprisingly, kept her mouth shut. Her silence made Christian looked at her sideways before he answered for both of them, saying, "Yeah, we are. And we want the kids to be in the wedding."

I raised my hand in protest. "A conversation for another time. I won't force them if they don't want to," I made clear.

"I'm willing to bet they will be in yours," Christian said smugly.

I nodded. "Oh, absolutely. Our kids are pushing for us to tie the knot. They made a presentation and everything about why they feel we should get married," I shared to irritate him. It was the truth, though. "Since they are excited about it, I'm sure they'd want to be a part of every aspect. However, we won't force them. You expect them to be mindless robots who follow all your commands with no feelings, opinions, or questions. That's why you get the response you get from the boys."

Christian pounded his fist on the table, scaring his lady. "No! It's because *you* make *me* the villain to *my* kids!"

Someone came to the table and set our orders before us. I corrected Christian as soon as the guy left. "No one talks bad about you but your sons. I have tried my best to defend you, but you keep piling shit on." Airen grabbed my knee since I was getting loud. "Christian, this is not a game nor a competition. If you treat your kids like actual people, talk to them, and hear them out, you may realize where you've disconnected with them."

He sucked his teeth. "There's no disconnect. It's y'all." He pointed at me and Airen.

Airen wiped his mouth with a napkin after eating some of my food. "All this finger-pointing is childish, man. I've had several conversations with your boys. Ashtyn is the one who's really hurt by how you handle them. No adult speaks negatively about you. We try to humanize you so that your son will also recognize you as a flawed human being, like all of us."

"Flawed?" Christian's head jerked back with an ugly scowl on his face. "You don't know shit about me."

Kaitlyn grabbed his arm. "Babe, that is not what the man said. Listen actively. We talked about this."

Christian snatched his arm from her grasp. "I don't need this nigga to tell me about my kids, Kaitlyn."

Christian's tightened mouth reminded me of how he used to think he put me in my place with that expression. By the looks of it, he may have already started his attempt to intimidate her. Kaitlyn looked at me with sorrow in her eyes. "How do we move past this? Like Khaliyah said, it's not a competition. We are here so the kids will have parents and stepparents working together to make things better for everyone."

"Fuck this. I didn't come here to be treated like some damn monster," Christian almost yelled.

His eyes tightened when he glanced briefly at me. I immediately assumed he recalled the time Aubrey had asked him if there was a monster that lived inside of him. It was one of many nights that he screamed two inches from my face after having a tantrum like a fucking toddler. Once she was about four, I didn't care to keep going above and beyond. If I didn't do things how he wanted or when, he had a tantrum. By that time, he didn't hide it behind closed doors anymore. The kids witnessed it often. They were happy we divorced.

Kaitlyn rolled her eyes. "I guess we aren't getting anywhere this way. Khaliyah, I am sorry for this and our first encounter. I hated you because of him. I had no right to come at you like I did, but you have to understand the picture he painted of you. If Christian and I can move past the lies and if he can finally let go of the past, we will have to start from scratch. All of us."

"Fuck you mean, if? Kaitlyn, it's not that serious. I'm still the same man. I saw things differently than she did. That doesn't mean it didn't happen. She's not blameless."

Kaitlyn turned toward him. "Your mask is off now, Christian. I need time to process that. I promised myself I'd never walk away from a marriage. I'm low-key glad we aren't married yet. This is a lot."

Kaitlyn's gaze fell on us. "I now understand he didn't want you to think you won the divorce. We had the ceremony with a family friend, but never actually got a license. He told me you'd come after my money by having the child support increased if we were officially married. The fact that you haven't attempted it all this time tells me everything." She shook her head and laughed. "I really came at you like I'd won a prize in his man. Seeing the damage in his relationship with his boys was a flag, but I listened to the lies. Talking to you, Khaliyah, did more good than not. I am beyond sorry for how I came at you."

I shrugged. "It's cool. You didn't know what you didn't know."

"But damn, I really took bitch to another level. You had me out here looking stupid as fuck," she told her man.

"You're the one telling all our damn business," he fussed.

"How long did you expect to drag me along without really marrying me? All because of your love of money."

"To be clear, I would never ask for more money. I don't

need Christian's money. It's his obligation to our kids. You never need to worry about that."

Airen nodded, hugging me from the side. "I can second that. Khaliyah and the kids are in very capable hands between the two of us. I will always provide for them."

"Sis, you have the man you finally deserve. I applaud you for keeping it classy when I deserved you to be just as ugly as I was to you. I am not this woman. I thought I was being down for my man."

"The fuck that supposed to mean?" Christian was now louder than any of us was comfortable with. "So, now I ain't shit. After everything I do for you, Kaitlyn? Stop playing the fucking victim. You wanted marriage more than I did. You pressed the issue."

Airen and I were low-key enjoying the show. Knowing what I knew now, I wasn't even mad at her. It was all on Christian. She had no obligation to him. She could run if she wanted to. She'd be an ally if she stayed. Possibly even someone I could trust because she was saner than I thought.

Kaitlyn told me and Airen goodbye and left the table. Christian looked dumbfounded until he noticed her walk toward the exit. He got up and ran after her.

Airen's head turned my way, and we stared at each other for a minute. There wasn't much to say after that disaster. However, it didn't ruin our appetite. We got our waitress's attention and ordered entrees and drinks. At least this disaster didn't ruin our night. Couldn't say the same for the not-so-married couple who left their food untouched and unpaid for.

THIRTY

Khaliyah

"Another vacation, Airen?" I asked him during our family meeting. The raised brows and sheepish expression weren't fooling anybody. When I saw my boys wearing the same look, I realized they had already talked about it. "Seriously?"

"Mom, please. You haven't heard where he wants to take us," Ashtyn raised prayer hands to his face.

Aydyn's feet tapped the floor. I lifted my chin and said through my teeth, "Okay, but it better not be another amusement park. I'm still recovering from the summer."

The boys' faces lit up. So did Airen's. He explained, "It's not until Spring Break. So we have some time. But there is only one day allotted for a theme park. You won't have to go if you don't want to."

"Good. Now, where are we supposed to be going in March?" I inquired to understand my kids' giddiness.

All three of them yelled, "Japan!"

"Oh, hell no! You know how long those flights are?"

"Mom!" Aydyn whined. "It's the anime capital of the world. We have to go."

"Besides, I already bought the tickets," Airen rushed under his breath.

"No, you didn't?" I pushed him from the side of me on the couch. "Babe?"

"Sorry. I got excited." He leaned his head on my shoulder before kissing it. "The good news is you won't be alone. The whole family is coming too."

I looked at him sideways. "Whole like who?"

Ashtyn answered, "PopPop, Gammy, Aunt Maya, and Uncle Rochon. Oh, and Aunt Karina."

"Karina? That heffa knew about this and didn't tell me."

Airen put his hand on his chest. "I made her promise not to. It's more of a surprise than a request."

"Airen Rochon!" I threw a pillow at him, inciting a pillow fight. Aydyn almost knocked Ariyah out, so she threw her pillow down and jumped on him.

I couldn't stop laughing at her throwing blows. Once Aydyn fought back, tickling her, she was done. Aubrey caught Airen off guard and got him right in the face. Her mouth made an "o" before she took off running. It didn't take long for him to catch her and tickle her to defeat.

We settled down before watching a movie in the theater. Airen and I were in the back alone. I leaned over to whisper, "How you gone plan a spring vacation and we haven't even made plans for the boys' birthdays or Christmas yet?"

Airen shrugged. "Ashtyn mentioned it and sent me down a rabbit hole while researching the possibility. Then I asked if the family wanted to join us if we went."

"Hmph! You're saying a lot of 'we' when the other half of the 'we' wasn't informed."

"It happened so fast, I didn't want you to shoot it down. I had to set it in stone first."

"You are so wrong for that."

He kissed my nose, then my lips. "There's one more thing," he said against my cheek.

My shoulders dropped. "What now?"

"Nick invited us to Aspen for Christmas."

"Colorado?"

"That's the one."

I thought about it for a minute. "I mean, it's not the worst idea. It'd be good to spend time with them before their family moves here next summer. Maybe we can all go since my cousin lives in Colorado. I bet Aunt Maya would love to spend Christmas all together."

Airen pressed his lips together, keeping his eyes everywhere but on me. "You already planned it, didn't you?" I asked.

"Kinda."

"Airen?!" I scooted over to the other side of my seat, farther from him. "I'm done with you."

"Baby, don't be like that. I know you are the planner, but so am I. It's okay. I got it this time around."

"Forget you," I told him before he pulled me by the waist until we were hip to hip.

"I love you." He poked out his bottom lip.

I crossed my arms over my chest. "Yeah, whatever."

"What about the boys' birthdays? You planned that too?"

"No! I mean, not really?" Airen said too slowly for comfort.

"So, what you're really saying is I'm no longer in the loop."

"Khaliyah, don't be like that." He laughed.

How was this even possible? Two years in a row, the boys asked Airen instead of me about birthday plans. We had two months to go, so I hadn't mentioned it yet.

Airen shared everything that had been in the works behind my back. Christmas was going to be two rental houses full of our family. All of my cousins and their families were coming. The boys chose an anime cosplay party at Airen's house. The boys could invite their friends to Airen's home this time around. He already had caterers and event planners on deck.

The only thing I was privy to was Thanksgiving. We'd be

hosting it at my place with the usual suspects. Izak planned to join us this year. At least I had input on one holiday. I was still mad, though.

"Kay, you don't have to do any of this on your own anymore. On the flip side, I now have a large family to plan things for. We can tag-team it."

"Okay, but don't leave me out again." I pouted and turned my nose up at him. "I don't like it."

After kissing my temple, he held me close. "I won't. I promise. We'll plan together."

We chilled in harmony for the rest of the movie. I couldn't really be mad at Airen for being all that I ever wanted in a man—one who was willingly involved in holiday and vacation planning. We really travelled together! It was something I'd always desired but rarely did before being with him.

By the time we tucked the kids in, we had a glass of wine before going our separate ways. The guest suite was my home away from home. We were adamant about waiting to do a little freaky sneaky until we shared the same last name.

With everything on our schedules, I was secretly happy he helped with planning events. August had us recording episodes weekly ahead of Grace and Lynne's show. A delay pushed their premiere date to after the holidays. For now, we talked about Fall shows, life, faith, and whatever ideas our team helped us come up with. The show was usually an hour long with no cameras. I was grateful for that one. Uncle Rochon built a dope studio set for us. Although no one would see it, it was absolutely camera-ready.

Business picked up enough for me to hire another programmer. I told Airen about the new hire. She was younger than I wanted, but even as a new grad, she was on her A-game. This new generation was something else. Her resume stood out with all the projects she'd done before and during school. She claimed to be an old soul who appreciated skill over sloppy shortcuts. The woman was good.

"As mad as I am that you left me out, I'm ready for a break. I hate that all of my work is in front of a screen. The plus side is getting to work for myself from home."

Airen swallowed his beer. "I thought August gave you office space in her building."

"She offered, but she won't let me pay for it. I told her not to treat me differently because of you. If I worked there, I'd be using the office for other clients' work, not just the projects she'd send me. Plus, I'd have two people with me."

He sucked his teeth. "Why you gotta be so damn stubborn all the time? Take the office, woman. We can go to work together."

"The construction isn't even done. You don't have a space there yet."

"Unc will finish by Christmas. We'll have a studio space to record our podcast. August also designed other spaces for different segments that she wants us to add on. The woman is finally using all the space she has in her building. I'm happy she at least did y'all's first. It gave me a glimpse of what ours could look like when we're all here using it."

"God seems to be all up and through this. The connections from you saying yes have set things in motion for many people, Airen."

"Hey, it's all for His glory in the end. As long as we do things with Him in mind, this can be the start of something so much bigger than us."

"I see it, babe. It's exciting."

"Once I learned to shut up and listen to the Holy Spirit, things began changing. I won't make that mistake again. Leaning on my understanding was the catalyst for the most painful lessons in my life. I finally feel like I'm on the right track. I'm not looking back."

"I heard that!"

THIRTY-ONE

Airen

On day four of our trip, I figured everyone would be exhausted. With more than half a day of flying on day one, we slept in and ventured out of our rental in the late afternoon. Technically, we left the States five days ago. We lost a day on the long flight and the time difference. We kept the itinerary light today.

The official day one didn't really count. Sunday was the big day when the men took the kids for an all-day amusement park adventure at Universal Studios Japan. The ladies went shopping, got pampered, and explored the city's cuisine and culture. Not one of them was up for lines and rides.

All we had on the schedule today were a few experiences inspired by IG suggestions and a stroll through a flower garden. It was a must for Khaliyah after all the research she'd done. We'd be traveling to another city tomorrow. Tokyo had too much to see. We'd have to come again.

The springtime was the best time for what Khaliyah looked forward to the most: seeing cherry blossoms in their homeland. Yoyogi Park was the showstopper today with all I had planned for my lady. Well, what everyone but Khaliyah had planned.

We'd have a photographer with us to take family photos with nature's scenery as the backdrop. Aunt Maya and Gammy cooked a huge breakfast this morning. They wanted to make it an entire day to remember. It would hopefully be the start of the rest of our lives together. We planned to dress alike in custom sweatsuits for the photoshoot. We scheduled it for the late afternoon.

At breakfast, I thought I'd be more nervous. Somehow, I was confident. I prayed about this move a lot in the past few months. I had the blessing of the Hobbs' patriarch. I had the blessing of the littlest ones in the Luke clan. All I had to do was express my desires to the one woman who changed my life with a single play date.

At the massive table, we shared our first meal of the day. I couldn't stop staring at Khaliyah, who sat opposite me. Our girls were on each side of her, and the boys were at my sides. Everyone at the table kept sharing similar looks since we were excited about today's events.

PopPop and Unc sat with me outside this morning as we had coffee for the day. I made mine iced and got clowned by the old heads. They both gave me marital advice that I'd probably need throughout my life with Khaliyah. They promised they'd be listening ears whenever I came to them about anything.

We played cards while my grandparent-safe playlist filled any silent moments. There weren't many. I learned where my lady got her trash-talking from—everyone who shared her DNA. The Black trivia games got us riled up. The men and women were neck and neck until Gammy, of all people, beat PopPop in the Black Twitter category.

"Y'all practiced that, hon! There's no way you knew that." PopPop was not accepting a fair win.

We had gotten so loud that the kids stopped playing their board game to watch and laugh at us. I'd grown to cherish moments like these. Before this phase in my life, I thought I had all the time in the world. Now, I realize how precious time spent with loved ones was.

It was time to get out of the house. We had at least three places we'd visit before the park. Khaliyah looked so good in her outfit. I pulled her into me and whispered in her ear, "Woman, I cannot wait until you have my last name. What these pants are making me want to do to you is unfair." I kissed the back of her neck, which I discovered was her spot a while ago. Her back arched, causing her ass to brush too closely against me. "Now you're teasing me."

Khaliyah turned around. "You started it. You must like the torture. I don't. I will bite you if you don't stop kissing my neck like that."

"I can't take it." I bit my bottom lip, teasing her back. She told me once how much that got to her, too.

"I hate you so much right now. We are not breaking our promise because you don't know how to look and not touch."

"Mmmhmm." I grabbed two handfuls of her soft ass and pulled her into me. Our lips pressed together for what felt like a minute. She folded first and parted my lips with her tongue. The taste of her mimosa still lingered. She sucked my tongue slowly and moaned needily. My dick fucking hurt, but I couldn't pull away.

For minutes, we breathed in each other's air, not caring about the pain we'd be in once we stopped. Her hands explored my skin beneath my shirt. Her nails gripped me every time she moaned. I slid my hand in her pants to feel the soft, bare skin of her plump cheeks. At that point, I wasn't sure if we'd make it to the aisle. If this were happening now, I'd regret nothing.

Knock! Knock! Knock!

"Mommy, I can't find my socks," Aubrey said on the other side of the door.

We were stuck in the same position, only our tongues broke away from the interruption.

"Okay, here I come," Khaliyah answered.

"Give me a few minutes and I'll make sure you do," I whispered while kissing her all over her face. I stopped at her lips and took the bottom one into my mouth.

Khaliyah pushed at my chest, putting space between us. "Mr. Landry, you need to stop. You are such a bad influence."

I gripped her ass to keep her place. "No," I whined. "I don't want you to go."

"Boy, stop playing. We have to. Everyone is probably ready and waiting for us."

"Let them wait. Just one time. We're getting married anyway."

Khaliyah burst out laughing. "You are a mess. Unhand me."

After one more kiss, I released her. When she turned to leave the room, I smacked her ass. "That's for my failed dick-satisfaction. He's mad at you."

"Well, he will be mad until there's a ring on this finger." She wiggled her ring finger before leaving the room.

"Woman, you just wait," I whispered.

"OKAY, now let me get one of all the couples," the photographer directed. She was an American black woman who lived in Japan. When she first arrived for the shoot, the boys had so many questions about what it was like living in this country. She cheerfully answered each one. Before we started, she mentioned that more of us should make the move. It's a better life, in her opinion.

We were at the end of the photoshoot. Khaliyah and I were the last shots of the day. Then we had ones with the kids. As the photographer directed the placement of the kids behind us, Khaliyah kept her eyes straight, ready to be directed. Karina distracted Khaliyah by coaching her to fix her hair. Then she came over to do it for her.

It was time for the shots. Everyone standing behind the photographer had their phones out. Khaliyah probably assumed they were taking photos, but they were each recording and would soon move to different spots to catch all angles.

"Okay, that's a wrap!" the photographer called out.

Khaliyah tried to move, but I kept her in place, holding her close. "I have a serious question for you."

"Okay."

I turned her around, pulled her into my chest for a hug, and spun her around so she could only see me. The kids were still behind her.

"What's next on your itinerary?"

"Maybe food. I'm kinda hungry."

"Food sounds good, but I meant on your life's itinerary. What is next for you?"

She looked at me like she didn't understand the question. I laughed at how adorable she was. Yet, she was also the sexiest woman in my world.

"What I mean is, I met this incredible woman almost two years ago. The first time I saw her, my daughter asked me if she could be her new mommy." She laughed at the memory. "Yeah, quite embarrassing. Over time, as we began with play-dates, I grew to understand precisely why Ariyah asked me such a question. She knew something I refused to believe. I shot down the idea immediately. I thought no woman could ever win my heart.

"It was essentially impossible since I'd claimed to have retired on love. I wanted no part of it after my first experience of what I thought it was. When I met a woman I can now say was created for me at this time in my life, I can admit how wrong I'd been. I recognized God in every aspect of my life, never my love life. He seemed to have just abandoned that part of me. Little did I know, I had to go through some trials for the sake of refining my thinking and my heart.

"If I hadn't, I would've missed out on the greatest love I'd ever experienced. The type that seemed impossible for me. The kind that included the expansion of my heart to take on a gorgeous, sweet, intelligent woman and three incredible children. A ready-made family. Literally all I thought I'd have by forty. My past convinced me it would never happen. But God kept me in such a way that I wouldn't miss it.

"Khaliyah, you are the result of what I thought were unanswered prayers for over a decade. You are everything I begged God for another woman to be. I've learned since then why I never experienced the manifestation when I wanted it. It was you. It's been you all along. We had to go through some tough lessons to perceive everything clearly.

"You are my family. Our children are siblings. And I am ready to do just what my daughter asked me to do in so many words when we met."

Khaliyah's tears kept coming, no matter how many times we swiped them away. She wiped mine from my cheeks before I slowly turned her around. She gasped when she saw the kids' backs. Their tops each had one word on them, from oldest to youngest.

Will. You. Marry. Me?

THIRTY-TWO

Airen

THREE MONTHS LATER...

As much as Khaliyah hated sports, she went all out with this NBA championship game party. We had a full house, and she stayed in the kitchen for hours prepping and cooking. The woman made me swear not to hire a caterer. She wanted to do it all on her own. She welcomed potluck-approved sides from certain family members.

The kids had the game playing upstairs on one TV and played games on the others. Khaliyah didn't allow them to eat upstairs, so the only time we saw our offspring was when they were hungry. My island was packed with food-warming trays and labels that Khaliyah was so proud of. It was professional chef-worthy. Her wings were always a favorite of mine.

The woman had potato salad, pigs in a blanket, home-made dips, four types of wings, a salad bar, and chicken salad. PopPop brought his brisket sliders, Maya brought several fruit trays and desserts, and Nina catered from O.C. BBQ because Khaliyah begged her to bring some po' boys. Nick's wife made cookies and brownies, mainly for the kids. Karina brought herself as per usual.

August and Matt walked in with their crew of boys. The couple carried in bags of liquor. No one was going to drink all that. One thing August would gladly do was let her hair down around people she trusted, then become loud as hell. Loud and so wrong. Watching sports with an intoxicated Auggie was definitely entertaining. I told Matt we had room for them to sleep it off if it came down to it. He laughed because we both knew it would.

Nina's sisters also came bearing gifts. Noelle learned how much Khaliyah loved boudin, especially boudin balls. The woman brought a bucket full of them with a variety of sauces. Lyric brought mixed drinks from her mom's business. August received her with open arms and wrapped them around the box Lyric carried instead of the woman herself.

Nina's oldest kids kept an eye on the classroom size we had in the game room. Khaliyah made sure there were plenty of toys for the smaller kids. Over time, she created a board game shelf that could keep any personality occupied. From card games to STEM activities, the woman had everyone covered. She also laid down the ground rules when everyone and their kids arrived.

Whenever a woman walked in and saw her engagement ring, it reminded us of the greatest day of my life. As if planned, they either pretended it blinded them or helped her hold her hand up because it had to be heavy, they'd say. It was the perfect size for the woman about to share my last name.

Noelle and Lyric's husbands had become new members of my tribe over the past few months. We'd met on many occasions, but Victor invited them over to hang out at my place when we played cards. Jamie was a fool. Elijah was much more laid back like me, although he was a former youth pastor. I stayed on my best behavior when he was in attendance.

The guys and I occupied the living room while the ladies hung out in the den. The game was on in both areas. A few bets were in action between the men, so the shit-talking was heavy in this close game. During a commercial break, I left the guys to check in on wifey.

Before I made it to her, she was walking toward me. The

smile on her face was all I desired to see for the rest of my days. "Hey, you!" she said when I pulled her into me in the foyer. "I was coming to check on you."

"Same. You good?" I asked, kissing her temple.

"I am. This is a great turnout. I love these women. But damn, we've got a lot of kids." We laughed at the truth.

"Yeah, we could definitely start a football team with all of them."

I couldn't help but place my lips on hers. The grin on Khaliyah's face exuded peace and joy. I had a hand in that. Happiness looked good on my wife-to-be. She definitely glowed.

"Oooh! Guess what?" she asked.

"Chicken butt."

Khaliyah rolled her eyes and giggled. "Shut up. Nina and her sisters are interested in joining our show. August talked to them about it a few minutes ago. She wants to make it similar to yours but with only women."

"Congratulations! Your show is about to really knock ours out of the water."

"I didn't say all that."

"The numbers don't lie. And as a faithful listener, you deserve it."

"The downside is that she wants us to be on camera now that our group is growing." Khaliyah pouted. She didn't want to be on camera any more than I did. "However, the bright side is that your people's show is almost over. So, at least we can stop talking about it and only focus on topics we care about."

I nodded and kissed her forehead. "True." I lowered myself a bit to look into her eyes. "You are truly a gem, baby. I can't believe you came so far out of your comfort zone for my sake. I know it wasn't easy."

Khaliyah shook her head. "No, the hell it wasn't. The

people who think Grace is right with her bitch-ass behavior on the show keep coming for me in the comments. I stopped reading them. They only have the narrative she skillfully created in her confessionals. I do not like that woman, Airen."

"You and me both. Lynne has been good with Ariyah, though."

"I know." She sweetly pouted again. "I love their relationship. Lynne's cool. Whenever I'm around her, she is super loving and kind. It was not the impression I assumed I'd get as your woman."

"Aht! My fiancée, babe. Get it right."

"Ugh, as your fiancée." She dangled her ring finger in my face. "No one will miss this thing. You hooked me. It's no secret."

"Then put some respect on it." I smacked her ass when she turned away from me.

"Boy!" She popped my arm before rushing into the kitchen. I grabbed her and picked her up. The woman was giggling like a kid. I loved seeing this part of her. She was far more playful than before. Whatever heavy loads she carried when we first met have definitely fallen off along the way to this phase of our relationship.

I put her down so she could tend to the food. I helped her refill trays she had extras for and wipe up a few drips and spills near the food warmers. The food was about two-thirds gone. She even had to-go containers laid out for our guests whenever they left. She announced earlier that everyone should take anything they wanted so that we wouldn't have too much waste.

I threw my towel in the sink and held my lady from behind. Khaliyah dropped her head back and pursed her lips for mine to connect. Once our lips touched, I cupped her chin with one hand and held onto her waist with the other. I pulled away. "I fucking love you, Khaliyah Landry."

The corners of her mouth made my favorite expression. Showing all her teeth, she said, "I love you more, Airen Landry."

After some music came on the TV, Khaliyah rolled her eyes. "Oh, great. There's Grace's show now. The finale is later this week. I ain't gonna lie, it's not a bad placement to play during a championship game. Clever bastards."

We laughed and watched along with the guys from the kitchen. The next episode of the Ex-Baller Family teased some drama of Grace and Lynne with other people. The shit was embarrassing. The woman arguing was Rondo's ex-wife, who agreed to do this show to piss off her ex-husband. Her words. Grace said something about me, rehashing old rumors for ratings. I was over it since we shut every lie down with the truth on Khaliyah's podcast.

When I looked up at the TV, whoever walked into the room surprised the women at the gathering. Lynne's mouth was on the floor. "Guess I'm late to the party!" I heard a familiar voice that hadn't entered my ears for over five years. I released Khaliyah and walked closer to the living room to make sure I wasn't tripping.

An older woman walked into view of the camera with the voiceover, "I'm Rochell Landry. Mother of retired NFL star Airen Landry. I'm here to set the record straight. He is not who you think he is."

To be continued...

Whew! Okay. I love you. Don't be mad at another pop-up character at the end. Khaliyah and Airen's story is about two people coming together and learning to fight what comes their way instead of each other. I hope that was made clear.

All or Nothing series has one more book coming. I hope you come back for the conclusion.

Thank you for your readership. It means the world to me. Please consider rating and/or writing a review for Back in the Game. I'd love to hear your thoughts.

I always have to thank my girls, Bridgette and Telicia. I will forever appreciate your support. Love you!

About the Author

Renée is from the best city on the planet—Houston. Since Texas is too damn hot, she now resides in Minnesota with her three kids. She writes fiction based on African American characters. Renée loves creating stories with relationship drama that can easily be found in many households. She wants readers to see themselves or recognize someone they know in her characters. If she can make you laugh, gasp, think, or even cry, then her mission will be accomplished.

Connect with Renée:
     On Instagram @reneeamoses
     On Facebook @authorramoses
     www.reneeamoses.com

Listen to Same Book, 3 Time Zones: A Black Book Review Podcast
     We read one book a month and post our discussion.
     www.sb3tzreviews.com

Signup for latest news, first looks, and exclusive content: bit.ly/RAMList

Books by Renée A. Moses

Turns in Love Series (Complete)
Two Lefts, One Right
Making a Hard Right
Straightaway
Wishing for Her (Christmas Short)
Truth Is...

Harris Sisters Series (Complete)
The Cost of Love You
I Thought I Knew You
Never Stopped Loving You
Not Good Enough For You
I Want It All With You

All or Nothing Series
Retired On Love
*Back in the Game**

Standalones
You Could Do Damage
When the Time is Wright (Christmas Novella)

www.ingramcontent.com/pod-product-compliance
Lightning Source LLC
Chambersburg PA
CBHW021328190726
48288CB00003B/1012